ONE MORE PUSH!

Close Encounters of The Midwife Kind

By

Sylvia Baddeley

ISBN-13: 9798388247469

While all the stories in this book are true, some names and identifying details have been changed to protect the privacy of the people involved. Any resemblance to actual persons living or dead is purely coincidental.

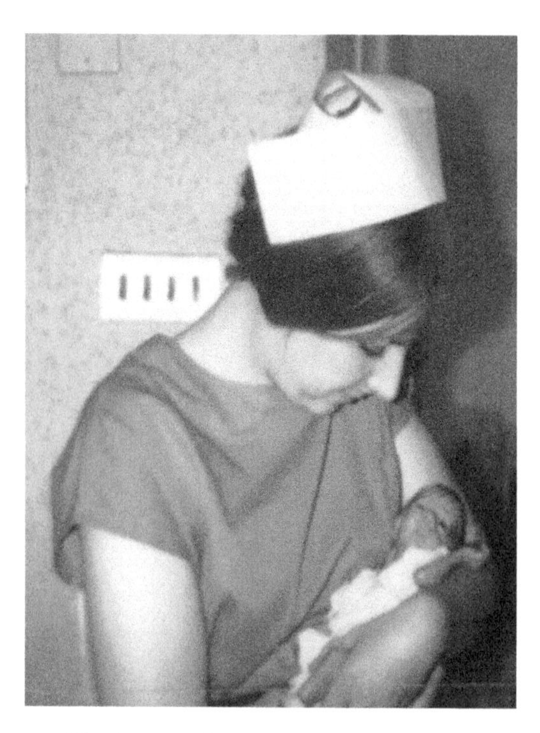

Working on the Special Care Baby Unit

ACKNOWLEDGEMENTS

I want to say a special thank you to William Cooke for his enduring patience with me, his eldest student I am sure! Your help and critical eye, Bill, have been invaluable and suggestions for improvement spot on every time. The Midwives of the Class of 72-74 (you know who you are) are deeply embedded in the reflections of my working life and will never be forgotten, especially those colleagues who are no longer with us. The many close encounters with women and families that I supported, and other clinical collaborations that I experienced so intimately with my colleagues, often when the going got tough, have sustained me with memories of a very special time in my life. Thank you.

CONTENTS

Foreword

One More Push! continues the story of *Push! Close Encounters of the Midwife Kind*, the first book in the series. It resumes the tale of young Midwives working in a busy West Midlands hospital in the 1970s where all of life's trials, tribulations, and joyous celebrations collide on a daily basis. Join Sylvia, Rosie, and Penny as they get to grips with their newly qualified status and learn what it's really like to practise Midwifery at the sharp end. Traumatic births, heart-warming encounters, and laugh-out-loud situations allow the reader to share their early experiences as they cope with ever more demanding cases.

Meet once more Sister Frenchit, who instils fear in the most stout–hearted, and the legendary Mrs Annie O'Neil, Senior Midwife Tutor who moulds naïve young women into competent professionals.

And finally, discover the secret lives of some of the main characters as you step into this vintage time capsule of one of the oldest professions in the world.

Chapter One

Sunlight streamed through the door's glass panel into the hallway, landing on the pile of mail that had just been delivered. Amongst the usual assortment of household bills and circulars was a rather large, thin, cardboard-backed white envelope addressed to a Miss Sylvia Ayres, with an official looking stamp on its top corner. The long-awaited day had arrived. The contents of the envelope would either confirm the determination and effort of two years of study or painfully dash the hopes of the recipient.

Sylvia heard the letterbox clatter as the mail was pushed through and felt sick to the pit of her stomach. She drew in a deep breath to try and control the avalanche of nerves that were playing havoc with her mind-set. The unbearable suspense of the last few weeks was almost over. Apprehension hovered like a big grey cloud and just the thought of failure brought tears to her eyes. Taking a deep breath, she swung her legs out of bed, pushed her feet into slippers, and made her way downstairs to the hallway.

Her mother was already up and heard her. She listened intently as her daughter's footsteps echoed on the stairs. Acutely aware of the importance of the moment, she waited a little while and heard nothing but an ominous silence. The silence grew. When she could bear it no longer, she opened the kitchen door quietly and found her daughter sitting on the bottom step of the stairs, clutching an envelope to her chest and quietly sobbing. Her shoulders heaved with the effort of trying not to make a sound and tears were dripping off the end of her nose. A lump formed in her mother's throat as her own tears formed and threatened to spill over.

She walked across the hallway and embraced her daughter.

'There, there now, come on, it's all right. You can always take it again remember, they said so.'

She crushed her daughter more closely to her chest and smoothed her hair gently.

'It's not the end of the world, you can resit, Mrs O'Neil said so.'

She turned her daughter's face upward, searching for more words of comfort and was stopped in her tracks by her daughter's response.

'Mum I passed! I passed!' and more sobbing ensued. 'Mum, I'm a Midwife!'

Sylvia's tears were joined by those of her mother's and no more words were needed. The local maternity unit would soon be employing the services of a fully-fledged, brand new staff Midwife called Sylvia Ayres.

Sylvia spent the rest of that day in a whirlwind of activities of which the first and most important was to contact the other students who had trained with her. That in itself was really worrying as she was dreading hearing that one of them had failed. All of her set had bonded completely with each other during their training as they struggled with the mountain of studying, assessments, and examinations. The thought that some of them may have to continue their life journey in a different direction was a possible, painful reality. She needn't have worried. Every single one of the eight students in her set had passed their examinations and were now *bona fide* qualified Midwives. She learned later that that was an achievement in itself as no other set in the maternity unit's history had ever all stayed the two years of training required to qualify, let alone achieve a one hundred per cent pass rate.

There was a plethora of paperwork to fill in and

individuals to contact that would formalise and trigger the employment of a new staff Midwife who would be working at one of the busiest maternity hospitals in the industrial heart of the Midlands. Qualifying meant a change of uniform from the mustard yellow dresses that direct entry students wore, to a newly introduced pale blue and white check model. Sylvia and the rest of her group needed to visit the sewing-room department in the grounds of the hospital. Every type of uniform required was originally made here, and she would be measured up for the new model, which denoted the rank of staff Midwife. Most of the workforce were not enamoured by the recent changes and preferred the more traditional uniform dress, but the synthetic nature and hardwearing fabric coupled, no doubt by the outsourcing and cheaper production costs offsite, swung the pendulum in its favour.

To have qualified and therefore been sanctioned to wear a blue and white uniform was viewed with a great sense of pride, but another just as important rite of passage for a newly qualified Midwife was the purchase of a State Certified Midwife Badge and a silver or silver-plated buckle, which would be sewn into place onto a piece of stiff, navy buckram that functioned as a belt. It was considered an important part of the ritual of entering one of the oldest professions in the world; the buying of that buckle, and the importance of its purchase was almost on a par with successfully passing the required examinations. There were many different styles to choose from, some antique, worn by nurses and Midwives from generations ago, and newer, more recently produced pieces that could be purchased from good quality jewellers. Sylvia had decided that with her very first pay packet she would find one that would become a constant reminder of achievement, as well as an integral part of her uniform.

The next day, Sylvia made the short journey to the sewing-room at the local hospital site. She recognised the ladies who had measured her up for her student Midwife uniform two years ago. Having assessed what size she was, they ordered her uniforms, which would be delivered to the basement of the hospital where she could collect them. The basement was where all the laundry for the maternity unit was processed. Porters would collect the hospital's dirty laundry from the ward areas in skips and it would be taken down to the basement level. From there it would be transported across the hospital site to the laundry department. Clean laundry supplies would be delivered back to the basement, including the staff's laundered uniforms. The pristine, white aprons and caps would be so starched they almost crackled when they were taken out and unfolded for use, and the recipient's name could be seen printed on the inside collar of the dresses.

Sylvia could hardly believe that two years had passed since she was last in the sewing-room, a little scared and wondering if she had made the right decision to train as a Midwife. She knew now that she most definitely had. Finally measured and sorted, she drove through the vast hospital complex of old Victorian buildings that stood on the former workhouse site and parked outside the six-storey Maternity Unit whose 1960s-style box shape stuck out like a sore thumb among them.

Discussions surrounding Sylvia's potential employment had occurred before the final assessment and examinations had taken place, and although preference of areas where individual Midwives would like to work had been voiced, it was well known that newly qualified Midwives worked where they were placed, grateful that employment had been offered whether it be working on the Labour Ward, postnatal floors, Special Care Baby Unit or antenatal floors. It was almost inconsequential where they were initially rostered to work as the first year of a newly qualified Midwife's working life was spent in a very structured journey, spending three months working in each area within the maternity hospital in order to further consolidate learning with practice.

Talk to any Midwfe worth her salt and she would tell anyone willing to listen that she only really started to learn after qualifying. This was also when the realisation hits home that Midwives were truly practitioners in their own right, making their own decisions and carrying them out without needing to ask permission from a doctor. This, of course, meant that Midwives were completely accountable for their decision-making. There could be no 'Well, the doctor told me to do it' or 'I was concerned, but the doctor said it would be alright'.

That weight of responsibility had been recognised early on by Sylvia and it had spurred her on to be meticulous in her record keeping, being very aware that if she didn't document fully all that happened during her care of a patient then technically a lawyer reviewing her clinical note keeping could later say, 'If it's not written down, it never happened'.

The Civil Liabilities Act was a legal recourse that parents could pursue if it was alleged that care fell below an acceptable standard. It implied that if a mother or baby was damaged, or died, through inadequate care or malpractice, the hospital and, or, Midwife, could be taken to court and sued for damages. Poor record keeping meant that a Midwife couldn't prove that she had acted clinically and professionally in the best interests of her patient. All records had to be kept for a minimum of twenty-five years, the time frame in which, if proven, parents could claim damages against the death of or damage to their child, and families could present a case following the death of a mother. This framework of accountability lay like a second skin over every Midwife's decisions and actions, and it was drummed into every student Midwife on almost a daily basis during their training.

Reflecting on this, Sylvia walked through the main entrance which was covered with a large canopy that not only protected visitor and patients alike from the ever-changing variables of the British weather but had also witnessed a number of births that had not quite made it to the Labour Ward. Deliveries of babies in the back seats of cars and ambulances as they pulled up outside the entrance to the maternity hospital were not uncommon. Midwives had also been seen on occasion rushing to the main car park at the side of the hospital where some mothers had misjudged the progress of their labour and their baby's Birth Book reflected in that, alongside details of weight, hair colour and birth marks, their place of delivery was recorded as the Maternity Unit's car park!

The main corridor as it was known was directly off the main entrance to the hospital and it was on these walls that a number of very large notice boards, with bulletins, staff placements, training days and dates and doctors' rotas, were placed and updated regularly. It was a busy area at the best of times as the corridor connected the hospital's entrance to the antenatal clinic. But now there was already quite a group of students standing in front of the boards, chatting noisily and studying intently the placement lists that would inform them where they would be working.

Sylvia joined the scrum and peered closely at the board. The Labour Ward! She had been assigned to work on the Labour Ward. It was one of her favourite places and she was pleased but also a bit fearful of the huge responsibility that would become a definite reality in just a few days. There would, of course, be many experienced senior clinicians and colleagues to call upon for advice and support, always available for a newly qualified Midwife, but she knew it was going to be another huge learning curve now that she was qualified.

She stepped back from the group and pushed through the adjacent large double doors that took her directly into the theatre and Labour Ward area. The duty rota, that showed days on duty for each Midwife on a weekly basis, was pinned onto another huge notice board that was sited by the Midwife station – a large desk area situated at the entrance to the Labour Ward.

The only analogy of its function that came to mind was that of a battle station meeting point. It was the engine room and control panel of the Labour Ward's eight rooms. The notice board housed not only Midwife shifts, but also those for Consultants, Registrars, Junior Housemen and medical students who were still in training. It also showed lists of Anaesthetists and Paediatricians on call for the Labour Ward.

On the desk stood an enormous leather-bound register that held hundreds of pages. Every single woman who delivered on the Labour Ward would have the details of her delivery recorded in the register and it was the responsibility of the Midwife who had delivered her to document the details. Each register was handwritten and the register was used for one year only; a new register was put in place on 1 January of each succeeding year. Between five and six thousand births a year were recorded in the register, which provided a valuable resource for delivery queries in the future.

Peering at the mass of information pinned on the board, Sylvia found the off-duty rota and studied it to see what shifts she would be working. There it was written in black and white for the very first time – Staff Midwife Ayres – and a brief burst of self-acclamation warmed her heart.

She would be working an early shift on her first day, starting at 7.30 am with a thirty-minute lunch break and finishing at 5 pm. Her working week would be forty hours in total, but she was already aware from her training experiences that often it would exceed that. There would be no extra payment given, but staff could request the time back if staffing levels permitted.

A voice hailed her and she turned around to see Sister Francis, covered in a green theatre gown with a theatre cap encasing her hair, waving at her from the theatre doors. She had been her Midwife mentor from her training days.

'Congratulations Staff Midwife Ayres,' she quipped with an emphasis on the 'Staff''. She was grinning from ear to ear.

'Well done and welcome back to the fold!'

Sylvia blushed furiously as a couple of other staff poked their heads around the door and echoed the same congratulations.

'Got to rush, we've got a retained placenta coming down from the top floor, will catch up later,' and with a flurry and a rustle of her green surgical gown she was gone.

Sylvia made a note of her shifts for her first week of duty and returned to her car, wondering, as she had done on her very first day of training, if she was up to it. The image of Mrs O'Neil, the Senior Midwife Tutor came to mind, who had instilled such confidence in her and her fellow students at their lowest moments. She recalled a conversation where she had said firmly to the group of young students in front of her, 'And if any of you are thinking of leaving you will come and see me first,' with a tone of voice that left no room for argument.

The thought of that encounter had been infinitely far worse than any other scenario she could think of at the time, Sylvia surmised, although Mrs O'Neil's bark was often worse than her bite. She recalled with admiration and awe the legendary reputation of the Senior Midwife Tutor who had been the driving force for hundreds of now qualified Midwives. She walked down the corridor, remembering how scared she had been on her first day as a student, how little she had known about women's lives then. She waved to one of the porters who shouted a cheery greeting as she made her way back to the car park. As she drove home, her thoughts turned to more mundane but just as important issues. She needed to buy a new pair of black lace-up shoes that would guarantee comfort for at least eight hours of a shift that was from now on going to become the routine of her every working day.

Chapter Two

The interior of the church was packed with family members accompanying the thirty young Midwives who were sitting in the first two rows of wooden pews. Sunlight illuminated the beauty of the stained-glass windows highlighting Saints from thousands of years ago. They smiled down on the groups of professional young women, who had scarcely trod their own paths of life and were yet to make their own mark on history.

The aroma of heavily scented flowers pervaded every part of the ancient church's interior, helped by the sun's heat on the old scarred brickwork. The ends of each pew had been decorated with fresh flowers by volunteers who had generously given of their time and money to make this service a very special day; a day that would be cherished and remembered. The symmetry of the rows of Midwives wearing their full-length navy cloaks lined in red gave a transitory illusion of a female Victorian gathering until the viewer noticed the white starched caps anchored neatly onto heads with uniform upswept hair styles pinned firmly into place.

The Reverend Stanley Smith stood at the back of the church checking for any latecomers and, when satisfied that everyone was present who should be, closed the great oak doors quietly and made his way down the central isle of the church to the pulpit at the front. The chatter quietened down and all eyes turned to the much-loved member of the church clergy who had officiated on many occasions in the local community. Stanley also officiated in the tiny Victorian church that was still standing in the grounds of the hospital complex, dwarfed by more recent modern buildings.

Stanley was kept busy with the business of pregnancy and birth. There were still a number of families who felt that a new mother and baby should be 'churched' after leaving the hospital and a simple blessing of the new family would be performed before the family went home. In more recent times, after the death of an infant families would request a memorial service for their beloved baby who only knew life on the inside of its mother's body. Stanley was very aware of the work of Midwives and the traumas that they and parents suffered when babies did not survive pregnancy or died shortly afterwards. He was the hospital's chaplain. Today's service would be very special, a celebration that had become a regular event for many groups of newly qualified Midwives.

'Today we meet in recognition of and give thanks for the work and support of Midwives. Not only for those here with us today but for all Midwives who work around the world. The word Midwife is no stranger to the biblical writing and teachings of all faiths through the ages. Every woman who bears the fruit of her womb has experienced the love and support of the wise woman of the community as she was often referred to, and today we celebrate and give thanks for these Midwives present; Midwives who have gathered here today to reflect upon their own journey as they step into the world of Midwifery practice.'

The church was silent. Every Midwife listened intently, many with tears in their eyes as prayers and readings were given. Finally, a table covered with purple velvet was placed at the side of the pulpit and a beautiful, chased silver bowl, decorated with cherubs and filled with holy water, was used to bless and anoint each Midwife's hands. They stood when called and, walking to the altar steps, individually received a blessing for the love and skill they were offering to women of the world. As Sylvia stood there, feeling the gentle trickle of water that was slowly poured over both of her hands from the symbolic silver jug, she couldn't hold back her tears any longer, especially when she heard her mother stifle her own sobbing just behind her. She felt that her chest would burst with pride and, bowing her head, the solemnity of the moment overcame her.

Then it was over. Hymns were sung, community announcements made and Midwives reunited with their family groups. The muted colours from the stained-glass windows created a warm glow inside the church's interior as the Reverend Smith offered refreshments at the back of the church and the Midwives and their families chattered excitedly, calling out greetings to friends old and new.

Sylvia stepped outside the door into the vestry. As she stood there quietly contemplating what had just taken place, Rosie Smith, her friend and fellow colleague throughout her training days, joined her.

They hugged each other, and a companionable silence settled onto them as they stood enjoying the warmth of the sun streaming through the open door of the church.

'Where are you going to be working Rosie?' asked Sylvia.

'On the antenatal floors with the dreaded Sister Frenchit,' said Rosie.

'That should be interesting,' laughed Sylvia. Throughout her training, she had heard numerous tales from students and trained staff alike about the regimentation of how Sister Frenchit ran her ward and her intense dislike of anyone and anything that interrupted its smooth running.

'I'll let you know,' joked Rosie. 'She's already talked to me about punctuality when I met her in the lift and I haven't even started yet!' They parted, promising to try and meet up when their shifts overlapped. They joined the throng of Midwives and their families who were now exiting the church, all chattering and laughing, exchanging fond farewells, and contemplating their future, as they both prepared to be thrust into Midwifery practice in one of the busiest maternity hospitals in the country.

Chapter Three

The Labour Ward was heaving at the seams with patients as Sylvia entered its doors on her very first shift. She hung her cloak on the already overcrowded coat pegs in the Midwives' sitting-room and joined a variety of staff clustered around the Midwife station, waiting to hear the report from the night staff who were about to go off duty. As well as junior and senior grades of Midwifery staff, there were Housemen, junior doctors who were experiencing obstetric practice for the first time, medical students who were training to become doctors, State Enrolled Nurses, student Midwives, nursery nurses and auxiliary nurses, as well as clerical staff who manned the phones, obtained test results and searched for patients' notes.

Sylvia joined the ever-expanding group of staff waiting to be given details of the day's work ahead of them. The handover from night shift to day staff was extremely important and it was after this had taken place that the workload was allocated to the various grades of staff.

She was incredibly nervous and felt like a student again. She smoothed invisible creases out of her starched crisp white apron and tucked a tendril of stray hair back behind her ear. The no jewellery, no rings (except for wedding rings) or wrist-watches rule was still applicable for all trained staff and she had checked she had removed her wrist-watch before pinning her fob watch onto the front of her uniform. Her stack of biros and the little notebook were in-situ in her dress pocket. She touched her gleaming new silver buckle, which had materialised as a surprise gift from her parents, gently rubbing its smooth silky surface like a talisman. Her palms were sweaty as she faced the imminent rite of passage of stepping over the line from student to practising Midwife.

Every one of the Labour Ward's eight rooms was full. If it remained that way there would be a bed vacancy problem later on in the day. There were six inductions of labour who had been started off on the antenatal floors with a Syntocinon drip and an ARM (artificial rupture of membranes) to help hurry along their labours who would by early afternoon be hopefully in the throes of established labour and be requiring a bed on either the Progress Department or the Labour Ward, depending on how fast their labour had progressed.

It was almost impossible to plan with any degree of accuracy what the bed vacancy requirements would be for any given day. Throughout any twenty-four hour period, women could be admitted in spontaneous labour from home, admitted for induction of labour because of a problem, admitted straight to the Labour Ward from the antenatal clinic if a problem requiring immediate action was diagnosed as well as transfers from the antenatal floors if one of their high-risk patients required 'specialling' or one-to-one care in a single room because of a life-threatening condition.

The large write-on wipe-off whiteboard, segmented into eight room spaces, that hung on the wall next to the duty rota board by the Midwife station was covered in code-like markings unintelligible to the uninitiated. Abbreviated obstetric problems next to a patient's name gave an overview at a glance of what was happening in that department. The Midwifery manager of the department had a grade description of Number Seven and she had overall responsibility and reported directly to the Head of Midwifery, meeting routinely to update her of any looming problems that the most Senior Midwife in the hospital was required to know about.

Her uniform was quite different: a tailored dark green dress which could easily be recognised from a distance, invaluable in an emergency.

Sister Stephanie Sparks was another key member of staff. Known as Sparkie for her bubbly personality and the verbal sparks that were shared with the poor souls who transgressed her high standards of care, she had been the Labour Ward co-ordinator for the whole of the night shift, looking after her own caseload of patients as well as receiving regular updates about every patient in each labour room. She acted as liaison, giving support and advice about clinical concerns to the Midwives on duty. She also worked closely with the on-call senior Registrar and Consultant Obstetrician on duty for the night shift.

Sylvia was in awe of her. The responsibility was enormous, as mistakes in observations or practice and not calling in medical aid or advice could result in the death of a mother or baby. That level of expertise and clinical competence took years of practice to achieve. She was about to hand over the care of women on the Labour Ward who the night duty staff had cared for to the day staff coming on duty. Without further preamble and not needing to refer to each woman's notes, so competent was she in knowing the detail of each patient's history, she launched into a comprehensive clinical résumé of each case to the multidisciplinary team standing in front of her.

'Right, Room One, a primigravida, spontaneous labour, progressing nicely, six centimetres dilated, membranes still intact, just had one dose of Pethidine, starting to use the Entonox.

'Room Two, thirty-four weeker, bleeding, placenta praevia grade three. Blood loss minimal at the moment, there's an IV in situ. We've notified the neonatal unit that we may need a place for the baby if the bleeding continues or baby's condition deteriorates, as we'll need to deliver fast. I've let theatre know about her, we've cross-matched her four units of blood and the Consultant knows about her too. Room Three, we have a breech presentation, five centimetres dilated, some meconium-stained liquor present, foetal heart recordings OK so far but obviously it's a concern. We have attached the monitor. She's being assessed by the Registrar now. Room Four houses a lady having her fifth baby, all previous normal deliveries.'

Sylvia listened intently as Sister Sparks almost without drawing breath gave a thorough report on every woman who occupied a bed on the Labour Ward. She demonstrated a complete grasp of every complex case that was that morning housed there and who had been under her care for the last ten hours.

The Labour Ward co-ordinator for the early shift was Sister Francis who had been Sylvia's mentor Midwife as a student. When the formal handing over of care and the keys to the DDA drugs cupboard was completed, staff were assigned to the cases they would be caring for on their shift. Sylvia was given the lady in Room One and she breathed an inward sigh of relief for a low-risk case, even though she knew it might not stay that way. She donned the obligatory plastic apron from the corridor walk-in store cupboard and put it on over her uniform apron. Pushing open the door of Room One, she smiled at her young patient and said, 'Hello, I'm Staff Nurse Ayres and I'll be looking after you and your baby.'

Sister Francis, taking over the care of one of her patients from the night staff and after introducing herself to the mother and her husband, arranged for Mercy to bring them both some tea and toast to boost their energy levels. Mercy was one of the Labour Ward's cleaners whose duties included the provision of tea and toast which was routinely offered to all newly delivered mums or mums whose energy levels were flagging. Mercy was probably not one of the qualities that was overly shared by its namesake as the cleaner was viewed as a bit of a battle-axe.

Underneath that forbidding exterior though was a heart of gold that once breached was as supportive as all the other members of the Labour Ward team.

Maggie, the patient, a relaxed cheerful soul, had been admitted in the early hours of the morning to the Progress department until labour had become more established. Sister Francis had examined her to verify at what stage of labour she had reached. She was still battling with a little niggle in the back of her mind that wouldn't go away. It wasn't that any complications had reared their head or that progress in labour wasn't being made. It was, but more slowly than Sister Francis had anticipated considering that the lady in front of her was having her fifth child. Usually women who embarked on fourth or fifth pregnancies that were problem-free tended to have rapid labours and deliveries, their bodies becoming more efficient at the job they were hormonally primed to fulfil with each successive pregnancy.

Peering intently at Maggie's notes in front of her, she started to read through the details of each previous birth, delving deeper into the bulging file of records that covered the last twelve years of the patient's obstetric history. She had delivered all of her previous babies in the same building that housed them both now and they had all been without exception very normal uncomplicated deliveries. She reread the course and outcome of four previous pregnancies and labours again and noted that all of her babies had weighed around seven pounds. Nothing uncomplicated or unusual about that, except that this baby, still housed inside its mother's womb, was quite a bit bigger, in fact a lot bigger. She closed the notes and walked over to the bed where her patient was lying and laid a hand onto her abdomen, keeping it there for a few minutes, assessing the length, strength and duration of the woman's contractions.

'Maggie, I'm just going to have a little feel of your baby to check how he's lying.'

She adjusted the sheet covering Maggie, exposing more of her grossly distended abdomen and placing both hands over her lower torso proceeded to palpate her uterus. Her fingers pushed gently into the distended flesh as she examined the contours of the baby's body. She slid her hands over to the left side of Maggie's abdomen, recognising the broad expanse of the baby's back and slid her hands down lower, searching for the baby's head. She couldn't feel any part of the baby's head because it was deeply engaged low down inside the bony structure of Maggie's pelvis. She placed her hands just below her rib cage and felt for the wide, soft mass that was the baby's bottom. Usually, when a baby settled into this position, the space beneath the mother's rib cage became a little less congested, giving mothers a little respite from the feeling of breathlessness created by the pregnant uterus that pushed internal organs and structures upwards. Sister Francis probed more deeply with her fingertips, noting how high up the top of the pregnant uterus still was in relation to the mother's rib cage. This baby was definitely larger than Maggie's previous four offspring.

Over the next hour Sister Francis was relieved to see Maggie's contractions became stronger and settle into a rhythm and rate that reassured her. She knew that once labour was firmly established, progress should be rapid for a woman who had previously delivered four babies vaginally. Once full dilatation was reached, the second stage of labour, the pushing stage, was usually very rapid indeed, involving just a few pushes. Aware that the second stage of labour was approaching, Sister Francis sent a healthcare assistant to bring Maggie's husband and then she prepared her delivery trolley. She opened up a normal delivery pack, removing the outer paper wrapping and sliding the sterile inner pack of instruments and fabric drapes that would ensure a clean delivery surface for the baby. She repeated the procedure, opening a pair of sterile rubber gloves and dropping the contents onto the delivery pack. A green, sterile surgeon's gown was added to the trolley. She looked up when the labour room door was pushed open and Sylvia popped her head around and said 'Shall I send Beryl in to give you a hand? It looks like baby is on his way.'

'Yes please, shouldn't be long now', and almost on cue Maggie uttered a long low guttural groan deep in her throat, a universal, well-recognised sign by Midwives that the second stage of labour had been reached. Sylvia went to find Beryl, the healthcare assistant, and Sister Francis busied herself for a few minutes, drawing up the phial of Syntometrine that would be given intramuscularly into the mother's thigh with the birth of the baby's shoulders. She checked quickly that the baby Resuscitaire was set up with all necessary instruments and packs that might be needed.

As she scrubbed up at the sink, the door was opened again heralding the arrival of Beryl who was to assist Sister Francis. A much-loved member of the Labour Ward and theatre staff, Beryl was an experienced, cheery soul. Hard-working, nothing was too much trouble and her amiable disposition lifted the spirits of staff and mothers alike. She helped Sister Francis into her theatre gown, tying up the back ties before turning to switch on the heater on the baby Resuscitaire and checking that the cot had a warm towel, a plastic cord clamp pack ready for use and two plastic name tags that would be attached, one each to baby's wrist and ankle.

Fully gowned and masked, Sister Francis stood at the right-hand side of her patient, swabbed her patient's perineal area to ensure a clean exit for baby and waited for what she anticipated to be a rapid delivery through a birth canal that had been stretched and primed by multiple previous pregnancies. Three contractions later with prominent anal distension heralding the presence of baby's head, Maggie put her chin onto her chest and needing no instruction or encouragement pushed long and hard. A thatch of dark wispy hair came into view and almost immediately the head crowned, controlled in its advance to the outside world by the guiding fingertips of Sister Francis's left hand.

She still marvelled at the power of the human body that could exert enough force to propel a baby into the world. To ensure that the baby's head was delivered slowly, controlling the pace of the release from moulding of the skull bones, a hand was kept in contact with baby's head. There was always a risk with the rapid delivery of a baby's head that the thin membranes covering the baby's brain could tear, causing an intravenous cranial bleed, and a controlled release from the internal pressures that were exerted upon the baby's head during delivery were an important part of achieving a safe delivery. The perineal skin between the entrance to the vagina and anal area was stretched very tightly as Sister Francis slowly and gently, to prevent tearing of the skin tissues, eased the head out, baby's face coming into view. She breathed a silent sigh of relief and waited for the next contraction and tell-tale signs that shoulder rotation had occurred. The contraction arrived. The shoulder rotation didn't.

The baby's head was huge in comparison to most of the forty-week gestation babies that Sister Francis had delivered over the years, giving an indication of the size of the body to follow. Sister Francis waited, mouth dry, her pulse rate matching that of the baby's 140 bpm as she waited again for signs that the normal mechanism of labour, where a baby's shoulders rotated slightly to align themselves with the position of its head, had occurred. It didn't happen. Maggie's contraction came, she pushed long and hard, her neck veins bulging with the effort. Nothing happened, nothing moved.

'Beryl, press the buzzer for help,' she called out, and as the emergency buzzer filled the room with its strident call for rapid aid, Sister Francis was already trying to slide two fingers down the side of the baby's neck, frantically trying to locate the top of a shoulder that would guide her fingers to the baby's armpit, allowing her to try and manipulate the shoulders into the correct position for delivery.

The baby's face was now navy blue in colour. Lack of oxygen caused by the tight compression of the baby's chest and cord in the birth canal was taking its rapid toll. Failure of the baby's shoulders to rotate and place them into a position that would allow the diameters of the shoulders to pass through and negotiate the angles of the pubic arch had resulted in shoulder dystocia. The baby was tightly jammed in the birth canal and the three-minute leeway before irreversible brain damage caused by anoxia or lack of oxygen occurred was rapidly diminishing.

'Beryl, get me a Paediatrician and another Midwife now!' she shouted as the door opened and one of Sister Francis's requirements was fulfilled immediately by the arrival of Sylvia.

'Shoulder dystocia,' said Sister Francis.

Sylvia understood immediately the enormity of the obstetric emergency. She felt sick with apprehension as the realisation of the perilous state of Maggie's baby hit her. Mouth dry with her own escalating levels of adrenaline, she joined Sister Francis at the side of the bed. Beryl almost ran from the room to find a Paediatrician and Sylvia joined Sister Francis in trying to reassure Maggie.

Sister Francis tried again to slide her fingers down past the baby's neck, fingers probing for the contours of the baby's armpit. She almost cried with relief when she found what she was seeking. She started to apply pressure, tugging and pushing the baby's shoulders into the position that usually happened spontaneously as part of the mechanism of a normal labour. She became aware of the arrival of other members of staff into the room, including the Paediatrician, and the sudden, stark contrast of silence as someone turned off the emergency buzzer.

She tried once more to deliver the shoulders, pulling down firmly on the baby's head and neck, very aware that the three-minute margin had been reached. Sweat was pouring off her.

The baby didn't budge.

'Sylvia, come over here and assist me.' A command, not a request.

Sylvia positioned herself on the other side of Maggie who was also bathed in sweat and looking distressed and fearful. She was well aware that something was wrong; her previous four deliveries had been nothing like this one.

'I want you to apply direct pressure over the Symphysis Pubis joint. Press down long and hard when I tell you, keep it going until I tell you to stop.'

Sylvia moved in close, placing one hand over the other and pressing down as instructed. Maggie cried out in distress as she increased the pressure and Sister Francis exhorted Maggie to push hard as she pulled down on the baby's neck. The baby's pallor was now a whitish, grey colour, signs of a severely anoxic baby. Sylvia carried on pushing down as Maggie shouted out as more pain than she thought she could bear enveloped her. All of Sylvia's reflexes were telling her to stop as she knew she was hurting her patient but she knew that the one and only chance of getting Maggie's baby out alive was carrying out the procedure that she was being instructed to perform.

The downward pressure exerted upon the Symphysis Pubis joint gave a tiny opportunity to increase the space beneath the pubic arch. One of the pregnancy hormones, Relaxin, affected ligaments and allowed more 'give' in the joints of the body, including those in the pelvis. Obstetrically this allowed for a little extra space within the bony pelvic girdle and was desirable. This last-ditch attempt to find more space to aid delivery of the shoulders was the last option available of giving any hope of the delivery of a live baby.

At first nothing happened and then slowly the top of baby's shoulder appeared as Sister Francis applied downward traction of baby's head and neck. She reversed her pulling and eased out the baby's other shoulder and lifted the baby onto the delivery bed as a rush of meconium-stained liquor drenched the bed linen baby was lying on. The Paediatrician was already waiting with a towel to take the baby. Sister Francis rapidly clamped the cord with instruments from her delivery pack and picked up the still severely anoxic baby who showed no signs of life. He displayed no muscle tone, his limbs were flaccid and he was making no respiratory efforts to breathe as she handed him over.

Sylvia was literally shaking in her shoes with relief at the delivery of the baby and couldn't imagine how Sister Francis was feeling. Maggie was crying, asking about her baby. Beryl who had arrived back with the Paediatrician was assisting him at the infant resuscitation unit.

The door opened again and another Paediatrician appeared who took over from Beryl. Sylvia comforted Maggie as Sister Francis with a seemingly unflappable calm finished the delivery of the placenta and was amazed and relieved to see that no sutures were required.

The Paediatricians were working frantically to resuscitate the baby for four minutes. A laryngoscope had been inserted down baby's throat and airways and a tiny plastic tube that was attached to an oxygen supply was pumping oxygen to the baby's lungs. Beryl had already contacted the Special Care Baby Unit, letting them know that a baby would need to be admitted.

The silence in the room was deafening. Sylvia's eyes met those of Sister Francis and Beryl, their masks concealing their true anguish. Sylvia's chest was so tight with tension she could hardly breathe. The only sound in the room was that of Maggie openly sobbing, the senior Paediatrician giving terse instructions to the more junior medic and the usually unnoticed tick of the clock on the labour room wall. Sylvia felt sick to the pit of her stomach and tried to stop her hands from shaking as she tried to comfort Maggie.

Both Paediatricians were bent over their little

patient, refusing to admit defeat, the more junior of the two fighting back his tears. A stethoscope applied over baby's chest was moved again, searching for the tell-tale signs of life. Suddenly, amazingly, there it was, irregular at first, then picking up in speed and rhythm as the baby's body started to respond to the life-giving oxygen being pushed into its tiny lungs. The baby's chest started to move as respiratory effort was established. The miraculous transformation from near death to pink-tinged healthy tissue and the vocal protestations of a baby trying to cry with a laryngoscope still in situ was like music to the ears of everyone in the room.

Maggie cried even harder. Beryl and Sylvia hugged her and Sister Francis slumped with relief, leaning over the bottom of the delivery bed. Sylvia had tears in her eyes and for the first time during her midwifery acquaintance, she noticed that Sister Francis did too. The Paediatrician removed the laryngoscope from baby's airways and carried on giving more oxygen via a face mask, alternately sucking out baby's airways with a tiny suction catheter. Ten minutes later, a robust cry announced to the world that a new baby was finally making its presence known and it was the most beautiful thing Sylvia thought she had ever heard. As the Paediatricians wrapped up baby and took him over to Maggie who cried again, this time tears of joy, Sylvia took her leave and returned to her own patient next door who was puffing away happily on the Entonox mask, unaware of the near tragedy next door that would define forever Sylvia's very first day as a qualified Midwife.

Meanwhile in another part of the hospital, Sylvia's friend Rosie Smith was about to experience her own rite of passage. The ward on the first storey was an antenatal floor. It had more beds than the other floors because the two end bays at each end of the ward housed an extra three beds, making a total of thirty-four beds.

All the women who were admitted onto this floor, and one other antenatal floor on the floor above, some for very extended stays of up to six months, had problems relating to their pregnancies. Three Consultant Obstetricians admitted their National Health Service patients into these beds and occasionally, private rooms patients too, as they were called, who received their antenatal care privately from the Consultants. All of the Consultants had their own 'rooms' or offices away from the hospital site and their patients, if they needed admitting, would be admitted to single side rooms if problems arose.

Sister Frenchit was the Senior Midwife who was in charge of the thirty-four beds which housed some of the most complex antenatal cases that were admitted to the maternity hospital. She was a petite, grey-haired woman in her fifty-fourth year. Tiny metal-framed glasses shielded her icy blue eyes, which missed nothing. A tight perm, long gone out of fashion, covered her head. She had rather lovely, relatively unlined skin and had she smiled she would have been considered an attractive woman. Unfortunately, she rarely if ever smiled.

She ruled her ward, patients and staff alike, in a super efficient manner that bordered almost on the obsessive. Report giving was expected to adhere to a strict routine of formality. Even the order in which information was given was expected to follow her instruction. Blood tests, X-rays, scan requests and a myriad of other tests and requests were filed with meticulous accuracy. Woe betide anyone, anyone, who made a transgression into the smooth running of her ward by incorrectly filing, losing or not obtaining the required information needed for the doctors' or especially Consultants' ward rounds. In her world, Consultants were revered, as was the controlled, efficient management of her department.

Her relationship with her patients wasn't much

better. The care they received was exemplary; no Supervisor of Midwives would ever find anything wrong with her practice. Her major flaw was her inability to demonstrate a bedside manner that made her approachable to her patients and many of her staff, especially the younger ones. Most of the patients who had problems would choose to tell the much more junior members of staff or even, on occasion, the cleaning ladies who had regular permanent ward placements, rather than risk the icy demeanour or less than sympathetic response from Sister Frenchit.

It was into this frighteningly efficient environment that Rosie Smith was thrust on her first day as a qualified Midwife. She had gathered with the rest of the day staff coming on duty at 7.30 in the morning, outside Sister Frenchit's office door. At 7.30 precisely, Sister Frenchit opened her door and allowed them to file in silently and pack into the small space. All were expected to stand throughout the thirty minutes or so that it would take for the night staff Midwife to give a comprehensive report on all the patients housed on the Ward.

Sister Frenchit's office, which was situated centrally on the main corridor that ran the length of the Antenatal Ward, was a place where only the invited ever dared to step over the threshold. Staff who were summoned inside rarely experienced a pleasant outcome; it was usually a discussion about a perceived misdemeanour from Sister Frenchit's perspective. There was no brief sharing of boxes of biscuits or chocolates that grateful patients had left on their discharge from the ward as was frequently had on other departments during a rare quiet moment. Sister Frenchit would hoard edible gifts in her office cupboard until Christmas Day and then distribute them solemnly, taking great care that due diligence in amount taken was adhered to.

Regardless of her personal traits which many Midwives and mothers found difficult, years later, conversations amongst staff would reveal that working on Sister Frenchit's ward had instilled in them superb work practices that had stayed with them for the rest of their careers. Though they viewed their placements with her often with great difficulty, they recognised the excellent organisational skills that she had bestowed upon them, skills that sustained them throughout their working life.

Having stepped onto the hallowed ground of the interior of Sister Frenchit's office, Rosie positioned herself near the back wall, waiting for the verbal report to begin and hoping fervently that she would be supported on her first day by the lovely smiling

Staff Midwife Hoolihan who was also sharing the early shift with her.

Back on the Labour Ward suite, Sylvia was deeply immersed in the care of her patient in Room One. Her pulse had just about returned to a normal rate and the contrast between Sister Francis's traumatic delivery and the calm atmosphere with a confident, relaxed mother was like a soothing balm to her recently frazzled nerves. It was her patient's first baby and her labour was progressing nicely. She was using the piped-in Entonox or laughing gas as it was commonly called, a mixture of oxygen and nitrous oxide used to aid pain relief during labour. Her twenty-year-old patient was breathing long and hard into the black rubber mask that she was holding over her nose and mouth, sucking in great mouthfuls of the mixture as her contraction reached a peak and then started to subside. She was beginning to sweat profusely as the room was very hot under the powerful lighting, and the physical exertion that her body was experiencing in the throes of advanced labour were akin to the amount of effort required to run a marathon, not as though her patient was aware of any of those facts or would have been interested if she had known. She had reached that point in her labour which was usually the most difficult for the majority of women.

She was almost fully dilated, almost ready for the pushing stage and beginning to feel some pressure that was telling her to bear down but the Midwife was telling her not to just yet. Her husband had gone home for a quick snack and a wash and shave as he had been with her from the early hours of the morning when her labour had started. The contractions were coming thick and fast now, one on top of another with little let-up in between. She tried to remember what she had been taught in the parentcraft classes but gave up as another powerful contraction had her grabbing wildly for the mask and crushing it to her face as the kindly Midwife caring for her did a very good job of rubbing her lower back and giving some much needed words of encouragement.

Sylvia's support staff, who had been popping in and out of Labour Wards One and Two, was Beryl. At Sylvia's request she grabbed a normal delivery pack and a pair of unopened sterile gloves and placed them onto the stainless-steel delivery trolley that was positioned next to the bed. Sylvia picked up her Pinards, a black plastic trumpet-shaped stethoscope used to listen to the baby's heartbeat. She placed the trumpet low down on the mother's abdomen and placed her ear onto it, listening intently and counting the baby's heart rate for a full minute. Satisfied that all was well, she recorded her findings on the labour chart inside the mother's set of notes that were lying on top of her bedside locker.

'It won't be long now, soon you can push. I'm just going to check that you are fully dilated which I think you are, and then we'll be on our way to getting this lovely baby of yours out.'

She went over to the sink and using taps that could be operated by hands or elbows, proceeded to scrub from elbow to fingertips using a bright pink antiseptic scrub called Chlorhexidine. Beryl expertly opened the pair of sterile rubber gloves and dropped them onto the sterile examination pack.

Sylvia undid the small packet of fine powder that was inside every pair of sterile gloves and dusted her hands before proceeding to employ the technique of correctly donning them. Her bare hands only ever touched the inside surface of the gloves; the correct technique for putting on a sterile pair of rubber gloves without desterilising them in the process had been instilled during her first year as a student Midwife and was so embedded after two years of continuous use, she hardly registered she was doing it, it had become so automatic.

She instructed her labouring mum, with Beryl's

help, to wriggle down the bed and Beryl removed the top sheet covering, exposing female anatomy that hormones had primed for labour and delivery.

Before Sylvia could perform an internal examination she was stopped in her tracks by what she saw. She was horrified to see a large white opaque membrane protruding from her patient's external genitalia. It was like a balloon and grew larger as Sylvia stood transfixed, baffled and concerned by what she was seeing.

'Beryl, press the buzzer for help,' she instructed, becoming more concerned by the minute. Beryl did as she was instructed and within seconds the Labour Ward door was pushed open by Sister Francis.

'You OK?'

'I'm not sure,' said Sylvia, casting anxious eyes at the balloon-like structure that was now bulging at the entrance to her patient's birth canal.

Sister Francis was smiling.

'Have you never seen this before?' she asked.

Sylvia shook her head, relieved that Sister Francis didn't seem in the slightest bit worried by what she was seeing.

'It's quite rare in these times of mass inductions of

labour. These membranes that make up the sack that baby grows in are still intact, and the pressure of baby's head pushing down now she's fully dilated are making the membranes balloon out with the pressure created by the contractions. It's very, very normal, just not seen very often.'

And almost as if on cue, the membranes burst with the built-up pressure of the contraction and clear liquor that was surrounding baby gushed out of the genital tract.

'There you are, normal as normal can be, text book. Looks like you are all going to have a lovely delivery,' and with that she left them to it, returning to her other patient, a high-risk delivery next door.

Generously lubricating her gloved hand, Sylvia centred her attention on reassuring her young patient as yet another powerful contraction rendered any conversation impossible. As the first-time mother-to-be inhaled deeply into the mask around her face Sylvia resumed the task of assessing how far on in labour her patient was. She gently inserted two fingers into the mother's birth canal and reached to the very back of the cavity, searching for the cervix that would inform her about her patient's progress in labour. As she had surmised, she was fully dilated, baby's head was low down, deeply embedded in the mother's pelvis. She ran her fingers over the baby's hard, bony skull, searching for suture lines and fontanels that would tell her exactly in what position the baby was lying. Direct Occipito Anterior her fingers told her, baby's head well flexed, chin on chest, the optimal diameter to pass through a normal size female pelvis which it had.

She withdrew her fingers.

'Fantastic, fully dilated, you can now push with each contraction,' said Sylvia, and with Beryl's help her patient was assisted into a more upright position ready to start an hour's worth of hard pushing.

Chapter Four

On Ward Fifty-Four, the antenatal ward that Rosie Smith had been assigned to, the workload of the day was well under way. The two student Midwives on duty that day were given the task of making and changing sheets on all of the thirty-four beds. With practice, it took fifty-five minutes and was carried out with the precision of a military tattoo If it wasn't performed correctly to exacting standards, Sister Frenchit's eagle eye would notice the out of alignment folded corner and make them do it again.

Rosie was given the task of the TPR round (temperature, pulse and respiration) where each patient's blood pressure would also be checked. All of this information would be recorded onto a chart hanging at the bottom of each patient's bed. Rosie was glad of the opportunity to be able to talk and give her patients some extra one-to-one care; something they got little enough of as visiting time was just for one hour in the afternoon and for an hour in the evening. It was also a legitimate way of finding out more about the women housed on the Ward.

She sighed with sympathy as she pumped up the portable sphygmomanometer to take a patient's blood pressure, because in the side room next door she could clearly hear Sister Frenchit giving one of the student Midwives a verbal lashing for 'ruining hospital property'. Apparently, as the students were getting to grips with the intricacies of changing the sheets, one of the bed chart holders had fallen off the bottom of the bed foot board onto the floor. The pregnant mum caught Rosie's eye and whispered,

'A right old battle axe, I can tell you!'

Rosie grinned and gave her a conspiratorial wink in return before continuing with her own marathon task.

When she had finished, she was assigned to work with Staff Midwife Hoolihan, the lovely Irish Midwife who seemed to have mastered the art of survival, as she had worked alongside Sister Frenchit for over a year, still seemed cheerful and yet was still practising Midwifery!

They were to be in charge of all the inductions planned for that morning. The ladies had been admitted the evening before so that at precisely nine o' clock in the morning, when the obstetric houseman did his rounds, a list of ladies would be prepped and ready for the induction procedure, which involved a full pubic shave and an enema and the insertion of an intravenous drip. Any potential embarrassment on the students' part, as it was they who were assigned the task of carrying out the shave and enema, was soon washed away, as it was a procedure viewed in the maternity hospital as common as taking a temperature.

Once the niceties of the pubic shave ritual were completed, a vaginal examination would take place and the bag of membranes inside the womb, encapsulating its contents, would be pierced. A thin, plastic stick with a hook on the end, called an Amnihook, was inserted into the neck of the womb, or cervix. The hook end would be guided through the neck of the womb and the bag of membrane holding the amniotic fluid would be punctured, releasing the fluid. Each patient would then have an intravenous drip inserted and a drug called Syntocinon would be added to the bag of fluid being slowly introduced into the woman's body via a cannula embedded into the back of her hand.

Stimulating a woman's contractions that hopefully progressed into established labour could be quite unpredictable. As Rosie accompanied the Houseman on his task of six ARMs (Artificial Rupture Of Membranes, or breaking of the bag of waters around baby), she knew her hands would be full with half-hourly, continuous assessments and documentation of her findings; all necessary as part of a Midwife's care during labour. It would be some hours yet, though, before most of these women's uteruses were stimulated enough to give up their contents.

Downstairs, in Room One on the Labour Ward, there was a uterus that was about ready to do just that. Sylvia was sweating now almost as much as her young patient. She had a plastic apron on over her starched one. The overhead adjustable light was powerful and emitted a lot of heat from its manoeuvrable mount. Her patient had been pushing for almost an hour and was becoming really tired with the exertion. Sylvia encouraged her through every push, wiping her brow with a cool face cloth, rubbing her lower back and changing pushing positions as her baby was descending through the birth canal well. Observing closely, Sylvia could see signs of a little anal pressure. Birth was imminent.

'Beryl, can you open the delivery pack for me, small size gloves? I think the heater over the cot is already switched on, but can you just check?'

Beryl didn't really need to be asked. Years of working on the Labour Ward and in the adjacent theatre had honed her supportive skills to perfection. Her presence at hundreds of deliveries had equipped her well. She started to prepare the delivery trolley.

Sylvia scrubbed up, repeating the thorough washing of her hands and forearms and donning a face mask. A sterile green surgical gown was ready for her on top of the trolley and after she thrust her hands into the arms, Beryl tied the fastenings down her back as she put on her gloves. The pushing had become almost continuous now, deep and guttural, a mother's body obeying its primal commands. A moment of panic from the young mother was calmed with quiet words of encouragement from Sylvia.

'Syntometrine drawn up.' This from Beryl who placed the cardboard container holding the intramuscular injection onto the side of the delivery trolley.

There was a knock on the door. It was pushed open a fraction as a voice said, 'Dad has arrived. I've put him in the waiting-room' and then it closed again.

While Beryl put a fluffy white towel into the cot under the heater, ready to receive the baby, Sylvia placed a hand onto her patient's abdomen, positioned the Pinards stethoscope and listened in to baby's heartbeat, as she had done after every contraction since full dilatation was confirmed. It was strong and steady, reassuring her that all was well.

Rosie meanwhile had just finished giving Sister Frenchit a verbal report on each of the ladies for induction on the Antenatal Ward. It was almost time for a fifteen-minute coffee break, taken down two flights of stairs in the basement coffee room, and Rosie was more than ready for it. Under the strict instruction of 'fifteen minutes and no more!' from Sister Frenchit, she walked into the room and was grateful there was no queue at the counter. She picked up her cup of coffee and plonked herself down at the nearest table. A familiar voiced hailed her and looking up she saw it was her friend Penny.

'How's it going on Stalag Fifty-Four?' she asked. 'Is Herr Frenchit still on good form?'

'You can say that again, she doesn't miss a trick! One of the new students was brave enough to stick her tongue out at her when she thought she wasn't looking. Unfortunately, she was by the big glass partitions by the day room, and she saw her in the reflection! If looks could kill, the student would be ten feet under by now!'

They both laughed, remembering their own trepidation of working on Sister Frenchit's ward. Penny was working on one of the postnatal wards now, with newly delivered mums and babies, and she was loving it. She had gained in confidence enormously throughout her two years of training and was still pinching herself after successfully completing it. Fifteen minutes just flew by and, fortified by the caffeine, both Midwives returned almost at a run to their respective wards.

Sylvia braced her legs for a more stable position and placed her left hand on top of baby's head as it slowly advanced from the warm cocoon of its mother's body. Powerful, muscular, uterine contractions, unstoppable in their primal function, pushed and squeezed a new life into the bright, noisy world of the labour room. Her pressure on the delicate head was light but firm, allowing the strength of contractions combined with the mother's pushing to slowly stretch the opening into the outside world, and allow the head to advance further and further. She was, by controlling the rate of advancement of the baby's head, reducing the risk of a rapid release of the moulding, as this could damage and tear membranes inside the baby's skull.

Moulding and overlapping of baby's skull bones

allowed adjustments of skull diameters as the baby had inched its way through the bony girdle of the mother's pelvis. Sylvia's control of the emerging head helped to ensure the smooth release of the overlapping scaffold of skull bones. She still marvelled at the processes taking place: the almost impossible way that the perineal skin stretched and thinned, under hormonal influence, to allow a baby to be born, and the way the muscles of the pelvic floor reacted during the second stage of labour to enhance the imminent birth.

'One more push, that's it, just one more,' urged Sylvia.

Chin on chest, her neck veins bulging with the effort of bearing down, and sweat clearly visible on her brow, the mother had her foot on Sylvia's hip, using her as a firm point to push against. With one last superhuman push, coupled with a triumphant cry, baby's head crowned, followed by a view of a little scrunched-up face

'Fantastic! Well done! Now try not to push while I just feel around baby's neck for any loops of cord.'

Sylvia felt around baby's neck with her fingers, and found a loop of cord which was loose. She expertly looped it back over baby's head and then encouraged mum to push once more with the next contraction.

With a hand resting on her patient's abdomen, Sylvia could feel the uterus beginning to contract again.

'Right, you've got another one coming. Here it comes, OK, push!'

She watched as the head slowly pivoted under its own steam to align itself with the shoulders, which were now lying in a position optimal for delivery, underneath the pubic arch. Another push and the baby's lovely plump body emerged with another gush of warm, amniotic fluid. Sylvia picked up the stainless steel cord clamps from the delivery trolley and used them to compress the blood vessels within the cord, sealing off any bleeding, whilst a plastic cord clamp was applied. Whilst she was doing this, lusty cries filled the labour room as Beryl said 'Syntometrine given with the anterior shoulder,' and 'you have a beautiful girl, beautiful!'

A warm towel was wrapped around a baby that was announcing its arrival in no uncertain terms. Sylvia handed baby over to mum who was wreathed in smiles of relief. She was overcome, eyes brimming and hugging her little one before planting a tender kiss onto a tiny nose. She asked the question then, that was built into the DNA of all newly delivered mothers.

'Is she alright?'

'Perfect, just perfect,' said Sylvia.

'Shall I go and get your husband now?' asked Beryl. 'And do you fancy a well-earned cup of tea and some toast?'

'Yes please,' came the reply, 'that would be lovely.'

Sylvia busied herself with the task of delivering the third stage of labour, ensuring that the placenta or afterbirth had separated from the inside of the uterus, now that it was no longer needed. The injection, given with the birth of baby's shoulders, was a drug that aided the contraction of the uterus and helped the process of the shearing off the placenta from the uterine wall.

The delivery of baby was 'text book' normal and, thankfully, so was the delivery of the placenta.

'And,' said Sylvia, 'not even a stitch needed!'

It was a perfect experience for her on her first day and Sylvia felt deeply satisfied as she finished her post-delivery observations of mum and baby. She checked the details with mum on the baby's birth tags, before attaching two of them, one to a little foot and the other to the baby's wrist and then, as Beryl went to fetch her patient's husband, proceeded to push her delivery trolley down the corridor to the nearest sluice for cleaning. On her way, she encountered one of the new student Midwives loitering and looking lost in the corridor outside the door. She looked petrified.

'Come with me,' she said, remembering her own very first day over two years ago, 'let's have a look at this placenta,' and together they entered the sluice.

Chapter Five

It cannot be said that Rosie was feeling the same sense of satisfaction that her friend on the Labour Ward was. The Consultant's Ward round was looming and Sister Frenchit was preparing for it. Every test, X-ray or scan result needed to be available and filed correctly, in the right place and in the correct patient's notes. She issued instructions left, right and centre, becoming more agitated and short-tempered by the minute. The Consultant who would be arriving on the Ward in a few minutes time was Mr Baxter and he disliked Sister Frenchit intensely. The feeling was mutual, but no way would Sister Frenchit allow how she felt get in the way of her own professional standards. She almost stood to attention as he arrived on the Ward, trailed by the usual crowd of junior doctors and medical students.

Mr Baxter was a tall man, the most senior of all the Consultant Obstetricians who worked in the hospital. Rosie had seen him before, as he regularly lectured to the more senior student Midwives about complications of pregnancy and labour. He wore gold rimmed, half-moon glasses, usually sited precariously on the end of his nose. His grey hair was thinning now, bearing witness to his more senior years. Always in a grey suit that hung off his lanky frame, his shirt at the back was frequently not tucked in. One could be mistaken for thinking of a benign professor as he paced up and down in the large classroom, shirt-tails out, but nothing could be further from the truth. He did not suffer fools gladly, was not a patient man, and seemed to delight in rubbing Sister Frenchit up the wrong way. He would ignore her, give instructions to the most junior of staff, deliberately bypassing her, and he would choose to look at a patient who was not scheduled to be seen, and not on Sister Frenchit's planned order of examinations.

Rosie was trying to keep out of the way as she knew how tense the Ward round could become. She sidestepped quietly in through the door of the sluice, pretending to check the twenty-four urine collection jars that stood in a long line on the work surface. Too late! She heard Sister Frenchit ask where she was and had no option but to step back outside and join the group by the desk.

'You can assist me on this Ward round staff, which

will be invaluable experience for when you have to manage your own Ward,' and she thrust a large pile of patients' notes into her arms.

As the group moved en masse down the corridor towards the first patient's room, Rosie trotted behind, clutching the notes and praying she did nothing to disgrace herself.

As the entourage turned into the nearest four-bedded room, Rosie suddenly realised that the Consultant was smoking a cigarette! His hand was down by his side, his first two fingers holding the cigarette, which emitted a thin curl of smoke. There were visitors' waiting-rooms on each ward where smoking was permitted but it was strictly confined to the places allocated for it. These were very well used and retained a continuous, smoky haze at all times of the day or night regardless of whether smokers were present or not. Rosie wondered if Sister Frenchit had noticed the cigarette in Mr Baxter's hand and realised she had not. She watched mesmerised and wondered how this particular scenario would pan out. She didn't have long to wait.

She was standing directly behind Mr Baxter, who turned around, handed her the cigarette and said 'hold that, will you' – a command not a request. He stepped forward to examine his patient while Rosie stood horrified, not knowing what to do next. She couldn't throw it away and she did not want Sister Frenchit to see what she was holding in case she thought it was her cigarette! A couple of the medical students had noticed what had happened, and one of them, who was obviously a smoker himself from the nicotine staining on his fingers, took pity on Rosie and with a wink, quietly took it from her, hiding it behind his back as Sister Frenchit discussed test results and reports with Mr Baxter. The life-saving medical student disappeared through the door, but not before she saw him take a quick drag on the Consultant's cigarette. He looked up and realised Rosie had seen him. He raised a finger to his lips, pleading for secrecy, and she smiled and gave him a quiet thumbs up.

After the terror of potentially being compromised and embarrassed in front of the medical fraternity had disappeared, a verbal telling-off from Sister Frenchit seemed a lot less of a problem and Rosie quite enjoyed the rest of the round. Even so, she gave a huge sigh of relief when it was over. She managed to replace all of the patients' files back in their correct place of filing, and had written copious test requests, to be actioned later, as the Consultant examined his patients and issued instructions about their care. Lunch-time couldn't come soon enough, and the care of the six induction ladies was handed over to another member of staff who had come on duty on a late shift.

Grabbing her cloak from the cupboard, she hurried down the stairs to the main reception area where she was lucky to meet up with Sylvia who was about to dash across to the staff canteen. Thirty minutes was allowed, to get there, queue for food, eat it and get back. Sister Frenchit had actually, pointedly, checked the time on her fob watch as she told her to go on her lunch break. They joined the queue at the staff canteen, bolted their food down and walked briskly back to the maternity unit.

'Well, there's one good thing about it,' muttered Sylvia.

'What's that?'

'We won't be putting much weight on at this rate!'

With a few minutes to spare, they noticed that as they walked under the canopy at the main entrance Sister Frenchit was standing at the window on her Ward, looking down at them, and pointing at her fob watch. As they rushed through the main entrance, quickening their pace until they were almost running, they breathlessly confirmed to each other that they would catch up, if they could, later on.

During the thirty minutes of Sylvia's absence, an avalanche of extra work had descended upon the Labour Ward suite of rooms. There were two trolleys parked up in the Progress corridor, one from the antenatal floors, as Sylvia recognised the Midwife who was bending over her patient, talking intently to her, trying to reassure her, from the snippets of conversation she was hearing. A member of ambulance staff who had transported his patient in from the community tended the other trolley. At the same time, the theatre doors were flung open to allow another trolley attended by two Midwives and a porter to be rapidly manoeuvred through, not deviating to the right as was usual, but entering the small anaesthetic room where patients were anaesthetised prior to their surgery.

The patient was on all fours on the trolley. Sister Francis had her arm underneath her patient whose modesty was covered by a sheet. Another Midwife was around the other side of the trolley trying to reassure the patient. Sid, a seasoned porter of many years, was manhandling the trolley with great alacrity through the theatre doors. Sylvia knew immediately what had happened. The most unusual position of the labouring woman on the trolley confirmed her suspicions. There were few reasons for a labouring woman to be in that position and all of them obstetric emergencies. It could only be a prolapsed cord. The lady on the trolley was the breech presentation case that had been mentioned in the report hours earlier.

A prolapsed cord was a nightmare scenario for Midwife and Obstetrician alike. The umbilical cord, the baby's lifeline for oxygen and nutrients, had fallen below the presenting part, usually the baby's head, but in this case, the baby's bottom. The cord had become trapped between the sidewall of the woman's pelvis and either the hard bony head or softer bottom. Each time a contraction occurred, the downward force would push the presenting part against the inner wall of the pelvic cavity, squashing the cord and cutting off the blood flow to baby. In the worst case, the cord could drop down so low that it became visible at the vulva, and the cooler temperature outside of the woman's body would make the blood vessels inside the cord go into spasm, reducing blood flow even more irrevocably. This, Sylvia learned later, was what had happened to Sister Francis's patient. The only course of action was an emergency Caesarean section, that is, if the baby could be kept alive long enough for the medical team to get the baby out.

Sister Francis's fingers were starting to feel numb and her back was killing her, as the porter pushed the trolley into theatre. When she had performed a vaginal examination to assess progress on her patient a few minutes ago, one of her worst nightmares was made real. The baby's foetal heart rate was very erratic and there was more meconium-stained liquor – a sure sign of foetal distress. She needed to check what was going on and an internal examination was needed. As she slid her gloved hand into the back of the woman's vagina, her fingers had immediately encountered the delicate coil of cord. She could feel through the thin skin covering the whole length of the cord the pulsating of blood through the veins and arteries in sync with baby's heartbeat.

She didn't need to count its rate or analyse its rhythms to know that the baby's life was slipping away unless he or she could be removed from the womb environment that was no longer safe or life-giving. The cord itself was covered in a thin friable membrane, a reminder of how delicate the balance between life and death sometimes could be during pregnancy. The softer tissues of a bottom did not provide the snug fit of a hard bony head within the pelvic cavity. Because the baby was smaller, due to prematurity, the loop of cord had slipped down into the mother's pelvis, becoming trapped between its hard sidewalls of the mother's pelvis and the baby's bottom.

Sister Francis had instructed her helper to press the emergency button on the wall next to the bed as she calmly instructed her patient to turn over onto all fours, hands and knees, whilst she kept her hand inside the woman's birth canal. It was imperative that if this baby was to survive, she must, for the next five minutes at least, take as much pressure off the cord from baby's bottom as possible. There was a five or six minute window where a baby was known to stand a chance of survival if it could be delivered in that time frame. She knew the theatre staff could get a baby out in six or seven minutes if all of the theatre staff were nearby and the one and only theatre was unoccupied. Miraculously, it was. The planned section for that morning hadn't arrived yet, for which Sister Francis was eternally grateful.

She was still bent over at the waist, calmly talking to the lady on the trolley and trying to ignore the pain in her fingers as controlled pandemonium in the theatre materialised into smooth, professional clinical excellence, as all the layers of staff, who needed no extraneous dialogue, performed a miracle that no member of the public would ever see. With ease, they manoeuvred Sister Francis's patient onto the steel theatre bed, helped her turn over, allowing Sister Francis to remove her fingers. The Anaesthetist was already injecting through the venous cannula in the woman's arm and preparing for rapid anaesthesia and intubation, as the Consultant Obstetrician started to swab the woman's abdomen with a bright pink antiseptic solution.

Sister Francis was still shaking with adrenaline as she left the theatre area and staggered into the nearest sluice to remove her blood and meconium-stained gloves and crumpled plastic apron. She leaned over the stainless-steel sink, taking some deep breaths, allowing the warm water to wash away the bodily fluids that gave a history of a baby's distress. The brief moment of quiet and peace allowed her to regain her sense of equilibrium; the sound of the running water and a few deep breaths restored, outwardly at least, the calm persona of a seasoned professional.

'Please God, things can only get better,' she mused as she went to join the throng of staff waiting for an update on the case and the never-ending task of recording in the patient's notes and documenting with meticulous care what her findings and actions had been. Just another day where a little life had been for a few minutes in the hands of the gods, as well as a Midwife's.

Chapter Six

The inductions of labour who had been admitted to the antenatal floor were all, without exception, experiencing contractions of varying strength and duration. Since returning from her lunch-break, Rosie had been run off her feet, moving from one woman to the next, carrying out half-hourly observations on their progress. Once she had worked her way through all six of them, it was time to start all over again. The bed situation on the Labour Ward was still dire and there was therefore no chance of getting any of them transferred downstairs to the Progress Department where their care would continue until they were almost ready to push. The less experienced Midwives would sometimes be lacking in their assessment of their patient's progress and the time needed to transfer them around the corner and, occasionally, deliveries took place on a trolley in the corridor. Sometimes, as the lifts were shared with visitors, there were problems transferring patients down from the antenatal wards as there was no room for a trolley and its accompanying staff. If time was of the essence and a swift transfer downstairs was required, Rosie had, on more than one occasion, asked visitors to get out of the lift.

The six patients who had been induced that morning all had varying reasons as to why an induction of labour was required. Three were seven days overdue and showing no signs of pending labour. One lady was severely hypertensive and had developed Pre-Eclamptic Toxaemia, commonly referred to as PET – a condition which, if not controlled, could threaten the life of both mother and baby, as an ever escalating high blood pressure and damage to the kidneys resulted in external and internal oedema in both bodies' tissues. If not recognised and kept under control, fitting could occur, caused by brain oedema; a very serious situation for the mother and the baby she carried.

The other two cases were as distressing to Rosie as they were to the mothers themselves. One mother's baby had suddenly died in utero at twenty-eight weeks of pregnancy. She had attended for her routine antenatal check, feeling healthy, blooming, excitedly anticipating her maternity leave which all women from twenty-eight weeks were entitled to. The

Midwife could not find her baby's heartbeat and her GP had sent her up to the hospital where they had confirmed that her baby had died. She too would have to suffer the pain and discomfort of hours of labour, sometimes for even longer than a woman who had gone into labour spontaneously, as a cervix or neck of the womb at twenty-eight weeks often needed extra hormonal priming to get it to release the contents of the womb it was guarding.

The other lady was almost full term. Her baby had been diagnosed with spina bifida and anencephaly of a severe form. The normal development of the spinal covering and the vault of the skull were incomplete, resulting in exposed spinal tissue, nerves and brain tissue. Many babies were not born alive as very severe forms were incompatible with life, but sometimes babies continued to grow and survive, right up to full term. As soon as they were diagnosed most women chose to have a termination of their pregnancy, but others did not because of religious or ethical beliefs. This case was particularly sad as the parents had already suffered three miscarriages and were desperate to have a baby.

Rosie couldn't imagine what the mother must be suffering, lying there in her white hospital gown, feeling her baby kicking and moving, as the autonomic nerve complex deep inside baby's brain still functioned, issuing automatic breathing responses. The trauma of knowing that her baby would probably survive for just a few minutes or hours after birth didn't seem fair. And how awful to have to be giving birth on the Labour Ward, hearing all the other babies, knowing that the room she would give birth in would never rejoice in that life-confirming sound of a baby crying.

An atmosphere of great sadness lay like a heavy blanket over Sandra's bed. Her husband, Michael, sat quietly at her side, holding her hand. There was little conversation between them and such an air of hopelessness that Rosie had to steel herself to manage her own emotions every time she went to see her patient. There was no checking of this baby's heartbeat every half an hour to reassure everyone that all was well, as it never would be. It drove the nail home deeper every time that Rosie went to her bedside to complete maternal observations. She fleetingly remembered an elderly neighbour stopping her in the street one day and saying 'What a lovely job you have, nursing all those lovely babies all day!'; a misconception held by many people who had no idea of what the role of the Midwife really entailed.

Rosie checked that the drip in her patient's arm

containing labour-stimulating drugs was still running at the prescribed drops per minute and made her as comfortable as she was able, plumping up her pillows and smoothing the bedcover over her distended abdomen. Reminding her to use her buzzer if she needed anything else, she walked from behind the curtains and carried on to her next patient who wanted to discuss baby names, and excitedly showed her nursery photos for their soon-to-be-arriving baby.

One floor below on the Labour Ward, Sylvia was helping Carmel, a seasoned Midwife of many years, to stock up the supplies for each labour room. Storage rooms opposite each labour room held boxes of equipment of varying sizes, each containing the myriad contents of what was needed to provide a comprehensive maternity and obstetric service to its clientele. Vaginal examination packs, delivery packs, different types of forceps, suturing packs for perineums that needed stitching after delivery, cord clamps, boxes of sterile gloves, antiseptic lotions; the list was endless. Making sure that each labour room had everything to hand for continuous shifts was an ongoing chore. Any time there was a moment to spare, stocks were checked and rechecked. It would be an unforgivable sin if, in the middle of incubating a baby that wasn't breathing, a Paediatrician did not have available suction equipment and instruments required immediately to resuscitate a newborn. Equally so for a Consultant who was trying to deliver a compound presentation, where a baby was reluctant to enter the extra-uterine world.

She had just put a stack of fluffy white towels onto the shelves when Sister Francis called out from the middle of the corridor.

'Is anyone free? I need some back up.'

Sylvia stuck her head out of the storage room and saw Sister Francis standing at the other end of the corridor and she responded with 'I am.'

'An ambulance is on its way. Grab your cloak, you are going to need it. I'm going to be collecting equipment and I'll see you in two minutes in Progress and will fill you in.' With that she disappeared, walking briskly towards the Progress Department. Mystified, Sylvia finished what she was doing, grabbed her cloak from the Midwives' sitting-room and made her way round the corner for her rendezvous with Sister Francis. As they lugged equipment towards the reception area where an ambulance would be waiting, she filled Sylvia in on the case details they had been called out to.

On one of the many notorious council estates in

the city, a lady with a twin pregnancy was experiencing contractions at thirty-five weeks. She was refusing to come into hospital. Her community Midwife had rung in for some extra support and advice after prolonged pleading had failed to convince her that delivering premature twins at home was not a good idea. Theatre, Special Care Baby Unit and the Consultant on call had all been notified.

Chapter Seven

The ambulance that would take them to their patient pulled up under the canopy and the back doors were flung open by the driver and his assistant, who helped them load their equipment. Sister Francis explained to the driver where they were going, and gave Sylvia some more details about the lady they were on their way to see.

She lived on the same estate that Sylvia had visited frequently when she was a student, experiencing her three-month, live-in community placement. This lady was pregnant for the sixth time with a multiple pregnancy, twins. Amazingly, because her records stated that she was grossly obese, her other pregnancies had been trouble-free, apart from some episodes of an elevated blood pressure. She had missed a few antenatal check-ups because she lived so far from the hospital, had no access to a car and couldn't afford the bus fare. Her local Midwife, who Sylvia had got to know well during her community placement, had tried to visit her at home, but frequently gained no access.

As they drove through streets of grim-looking council houses, many unkempt and in dire need of renovation, Sylvia reflected upon the many cases she had visited in situations akin to the one they were about to call on. Working inside the hospital was so very different. There was a perceived hierarchy whereby anyone with a uniform on was at least listened to and respected for their professional status. Patients were out of their home environment and felt vulnerable, and apart from drunk, aggressive husbands or boyfriends, patients were usually compliant in even the most difficult of circumstances. However, working in the community meant that you were beholden to householders to let you in through the front door. You were firmly on their territory. There was no hiding behind the authority of a uniform or doctor's white coat.

The ambulance pulled up outside the council house behind a car that Sylvia recognised as Gwyneth's, one of the community Midwives. The front door opened and Gwyneth greeted them, looking relieved.

'She's through here, this way,' and they all trooped

down a small passageway that opened out into one of the most chaotic scenes Sylvia had ever seen.

The room was dominated by the presence of a very large bed taking up most of the available floor space. An enormous television was perched on top of a battered-looking chest of drawers and it was turned on at a volume that even the hard of hearing would have no difficulty in understanding. What little furniture there was, was covered in a jumble of clothes, toys and piles of magazines. There were overflowing waste bins and a few unwashed plates and utensils from a recent meal of curry, whose pungent aroma pervaded every part of the room.

Sitting like a queen on a throne in the centre of the bed was the pregnant lady in question. Her bulk and girth were spectacular. Sylvia had never seen anyone so overweight in her life. How on earth anyone had managed to palpate a pregnant uterus through the mounds of flesh that were in the way was beyond her. She fleetingly thought about the baby's moment of conception and the challenges of the act of copulation and rapidly chose not to pursue that line of thought any longer!

Charlene, Sylvia mused silently, must have been in the twenty-four stone category. She was short in stature, with very long, straight hair tinged with grey and parted in the middle. Her large round face was extremely puffy, almost obscuring her eyes, and she was wearing a huge multicoloured kaftan that just about covered her bulk. On the bed with her were three of her youngest brood, ranging in age from eighteen months to four years. At the bottom of the bed, a whippet obviously used to living in a permanent state of mayhem lay unperturbed, curled up, fast asleep and snoring. To make matters worse, three individuals who turned out to be friends and neighbours, were sitting either side of the bed. It was almost impossible to squeeze anybody else into the space. Sister Francis took control.

'Right ladies, can I ask you to vacate to another room whilst we examine Charlene? And I would be grateful if you could turn the TV's volume down a bit.' This was declared in a forthright, no-nonsense request that dared the recipients not to comply.

With a load of muttering and grumbling, Charlene's neighbours noisily pushed their chairs back and squeezed past the Midwives into the hall, forgetting to turn the TV's volume down on their way out. This was left to Sylvia, who shuffled around the room's cramped interior to reach the TV and rectify the volume, as Gwyneth introduced Sister Francis.

Gwyneth then settled Charlene into a half-lying position and placed her hands onto her exposed abdomen. Almost on cue, Charlene gave a little grimace of discomfort as a contraction started to build. There was no mistaking what she was feeling; labour was threatening to expel two little ones who needed a few weeks more of growth and development inside their mother's body. Gwyneth kept her hands where they were, and felt three more weak and short, but regular contractions.

'Charlene, my love, these tightenings are more regular now. We really need to get you into hospital. This is no place for your babies, who will be premature, to be born.'

'I can't see what all the fuss is about,' said Charlene. 'All my other babies have been normal. I ain't 'ad no problems with them so why should I have any with these?'

'All your other babies were on time, they weren't premature, and this time you have two babies in there, one of which is not lying in a head-down position. It's lying right across the other which means you might not have normal deliveries. And that's not taking into account that your babies' lungs will not be fully mature. If we get you in and try and stop the contractions, it will give time for the babies' lungs to mature a bit longer.'

Charlene resolutely refused to budge.

'Anyway, I've got nobody to look after the kids or sort their teas,' and she looked fondly at her brood who were completely unfazed by the goings-on around them, playing together at the bottom of the bed.

Whilst Gwyneth tried to persuade Charlene further, Sister Francis went outside and updated the ambulance staff who were patiently waiting, grateful for a cigarette break by the roadside. By now, all the neighbours had noticed the arrival of the ambulance and a small crowd was gathering, kids in tow.

Sister Francis returned to the front room and tried another persuasive tack.

'Charlene … would you like a completely pain-free labour with no discomfort at all? I know your other babies were all normal deliveries, but your last labour was a long one and you needed extra pain relief, didn't you?'

Charlene nodded, and groaned again as another contraction reared its head. It seemed that even in the last half an hour, the contractions were accelerating.

'… if we get you in, in time, we can get an epidural

put in. You've heard about those, haven't you?'

Charlene looked puzzled. She had never heard of an epidural. She had never attended any parentcraft classes even though there was a class almost on her doorstep. Her mother had said they were a waste of time, and what was good enough for her mother was good enough for her. Being pregnant for most of her married life was a completely normal way to live, as it had been for her mother, who had borne ten children.

Another contraction assaulted her body, and this time she gasped with pain. For the first time, she looked a bit unsure, and her cocky self-confidence diminished.

'I think we'd better examine you and see what's going on down there,' said Sister Francis. 'Which way is the sink?'

Gwyneth pointed the way, and continued to press home Sister Francis' cajoling as Sylvia followed Sister Francis down the hallway to the kitchen.

The kitchen was a mirror image of the front room, minus the bed. Contents that would usually be stored out of sight in cupboards, sideboards, or chests of drawers were stacked wherever there was a space to put anything. A battered table with a motley collection of mismatched chairs was stacked with dishes that needed washing. The sink and draining board were similarly adorned with used and dirty tableware. It was quite difficult to get to the taps as the pile of dishes was so high, but with some deft manoeuvring, Sister Francis managed to wash her hands with a bit of soap she found on the side of the draining board. She looked at the state of the only towel she could see, hanging off a nail on the back door, and patted them dry on the side of her uniform dress instead.

In the front room, Gwyneth had managed to make some room on the bed and had opened up a vaginal delivery pack. Sister Francis donned a sterile pair of gloves and sat on the side of the bed whilst Sylvia and Gwyneth pulled the sheets and blankets down, exposing Charlene's genital area. Very gently, avoiding as little stimulation of the neck of the womb as possible, she inserted her fingers and felt for the cervix at the back of the vagina. She found the entrance to the womb with little difficulty. This birth canal had been stretched by multiple pregnancies and the pelvic floor musculature was quite lax. Five centimetres, and thin. Time was of the essence. Experience and previous pregnancies told her that this lady would labour very quickly indeed. She carefully withdrew her fingers and said, as another contraction primed the uterine muscle into action:

'Right then, are we taking you in? Do you fancy an epidural?' The timing of the question, as the contraction built, was instrumental in changing Charlene's mind.

'Yes,' she gasped. 'Yes!'

Gwyneth, who knew most of the neighbours because she had either delivered or cared for them, went and asked if any of them would be willing to look after the children until Charlene's husband came home from his shift at the pit. The lady who lived next door said, 'No problem ducks, they almost live at my house, anyway, playing with my nippers. They'll be safe with me,' at which Charlene gasped out her thanks as she was assaulted by yet another contraction.

Sister Francis went outside to speak to the ambulance staff.

'Right lads, we've got twins, premature labour, abnormal position. Labour is going to be quick and she can't be delivering here and definitely not in the back of the ambulance. We need a fast transfer and I'll bleep the Labour Ward to tell them we are on our way with her.' She went into the house and the ambulance driver and his colleague proceeded to get the stretcher. They encountered a problem as soon as they attempted to get through the front door. The turning angle and space that was available was just too tight; there was no way the patient was coming out that way on a stretcher. They returned to their vehicle and came back with a wheelchair. By this time the crowd in the street was bigger, with an almost party-like atmosphere, as out-of-work neighbours and children settled in for goings-on that were better viewing than Coronation Street.

Getting Charlene into the wheelchair was also proving difficult. Her sheer weight and size made manoeuvres very difficult indeed. There was a lot of pulling, pushing and supporting. At one point, Sylvia was almost squashed flat as she knelt on the other side of the bed, next to Charlene, trying to help her turn sideways so she could get into the wheelchair. Charlene lost her balance when another contraction made its entrance, and it was only the Olympian efforts of the ambulance driver who saved Sylvia from injuries that could have resulted in a visit to the accident and emergency department!

At last, their patient was in the wheelchair, which groaned and protested at the weight of its passenger. Manoeuvring it and its occupant out of the house was a feat of dexterity and strength that deserved a medal but finally, the sweating, out-of-breath ambulance staff had Charlene firmly strapped into the trolley in the back of the ambulance.

Sister Francis and Sylvia climbed in the back with her, and as the doors clanged shut, reassured their charge that she would soon be safe at the hospital.

'I've changed my mi…' Charlene's comment was fortunately unfinished as she was wracked with another contraction.

Sister Francis chose not to hear what her patient was trying to say and shouted to the front of the ambulance, 'Put your foot down, lads, as quick as you can now.'

With no more ado, the ambulance's lights and siren were activated and the increased acceleration almost knocked Sylvia off the side seat onto the floor. There were leather straps hanging down from the roof, meant for hanging onto and stabilising bodies that were inside an ambulance being driven like a car in the Monte Carlo rally, and Sylvia hung on, grateful for the extra stability they gave her. Trying to stay upright, Sister Francis asked the other ambulance staff to put a call through to the Labour Ward and tell them they might want to get theatre ready as it was going to be a close call.

Charlene's contractions were coming thick and fast

now, and Sister Francis knew there would be no chance of getting an epidural put in before delivery. Both Midwives inwardly prayed that Charlene's waters would not break, as that event often stimulated labour even more and there was the added danger in this situation of another prolapsed cord, which, if it occurred, God forbid, would break the maternity hospital's record of the same Midwife dealing with two prolapsed cords on one day – an honour that Sister Francis most definitely did not want to achieve.

'I want to push,' said Charlene.

They were less than a mile from the hospital.

'Charlene, my love, don't push. Look at me and listen. Come on, look at me,' and Sister Francis gave the quickest lesson ever in controlled breathing to help Charlene control the urges of her contractions. She was on her knees on the hard ambulance floor and had been in that position for the last ten minutes, encouraging Charlene with her attempts not to push. Her knees were bruised and were killing her. She hoped she had a spare pair of tights in her locker. The ambulance entered the hospital gates, almost on two wheels, and a few seconds later pulled up under the entrance canopy. There were three members of medical staff and a trolley waiting for them – a glorious sight! The back doors of the ambulance were flung open and the patient rapidly offloaded onto the hospital trolley. At almost a run, the trolley was pushed down the corridor and into the open doors of the theatre.

'Thanks lads, you did a brilliant job. Couldn't have made it without you, and I definitely think you could win Le Mans if you entered!'

'All in a day's work, sister,' they replied.

Sister Francis looked at Sylvia and said, 'I need to go and write up the records. Do you fancy some tea and toast? I think we just earned it.'

And so the restorative qualities of tea and toast from Mercy's kitchen once more came to the rescue as they returned to the Labour Ward and the friendly jibes from their colleagues of 'Been shopping, you two? What took you so long!'

Chapter Eight

While Sylvia was hanging on for dear life in the back of an ambulance, Rosie was looking forward to the end of her shift. Two of the ladies who had been induced for being a week overdue had been transferred downstairs to the Progress Department as their labours were progressing. Two more needed to be sent downstairs as they had been confirmed to be in established labour but, at present, there were no available beds for them. They were still comfortable, all observations were within normal limits, and so they were to remain upstairs on the antenatal floor for a little while longer.

She walked down the corridor for the umpteenth time that day and entered the four-bedded room where some of the ladies for induction had been warded. The bed nearest the window had its curtains drawn around it, trying, and failing, to give its occupant some privacy and distance from the promise of new life soon to be realised by the other three occupants. The thin veneer of curtain between the woman in the bed and the other mothers–to-be in the room did nothing to diminish the deep-seated grief that was threatening to engulf her.

When they had told her that her baby had died at her twenty-eight week check-up, she had refused to believe them.

'That can't be right, I felt baby moving this morning. That just can't be right.' A steel fist had closed around her chest, compressing tighter and tighter, as the Obstetrician explained gently that there was no mistake. Often, movement of the womb itself in the pelvic cavity was mistaken for movements of the baby. Her husband, mother, family and friends had all been devastated, and expressed their emotions freely, crying, hugging each other and using each other for support in a way that she found impossible to draw strength from.

She had not cried. She had become emotionally isolated, self-inflicted in an attempt to keep a distance from the harsh truth of reality. She wouldn't, couldn't talk to anyone, not even her husband whose suffering was evident in his red-rimmed eyes and loss of weight. She could hear the visitors of the other women being induced, excited, planning celebrations, knowing that at some time soon, a new member of their family would be there at their bedsides. She blocked out any conversation and turned onto her side, facing the wall.

This was how Rosie found her a short while later as she completed her observations and asked her to turn over. She placed a hand onto her abdomen and timed the contractions of the woman whose name was Helen. She had given her many opportunities to talk but she had accepted none of the support being offered. Rosie had voiced her worries to Staff Nurse Hoolihan, the lovely Irish, more experienced Midwife who had worked for over a year on the antenatal floor, and who had looked after a number of ladies in the same, sad situation. She had patiently explained that women who had been diagnosed with an Intrauterine Death reacted and grieved for their loss in many different ways and over very different time frames. She would reach out when she was ready, and for some women that could be weeks or even months.

Reassured she was doing the best she could for her patient, Rosie had concentrated on keeping her comfortable, and making sure she had her buzzer to hand in case she needed anything. Helen's contractions were becoming longer and stronger and Rosie knew that very soon she would need to be transferred downstairs. She walked back up the corridor and rang the Labour Ward to see if there were any beds free. She was lucky for one had just been vacated and was in the process of being cleaned. She updated Staff Hoolihan and, returning to Helen's bedside, informed her that a transfer downstairs to the Labour Ward had been arranged.

For the first time in two weeks, Helen roused herself from the grey fog of lethargy that she had been trapped in and asked Rosie to repeat what she had just said. As she did so, a shudder took hold of her whole body. For the first time, tears appeared and ran down, covering the chalk-white cheeks and cracked lips.

'I can't,' she whispered, 'I can't do it.' A fine quiver ran through her body and she suddenly seemed to collapse like a deflated balloon, isolated in her crumpled bed sheets.

Rosie leaned over and hugged her. She didn't care if Sister Frenchit, who would have been appalled at this level of unprofessional contact, saw her. She recognised the emotional breakdown of her patient and knew that what she needed more than anything to allay the fear and distress was human, loving contact. They clung to each other fiercely, one giving, one receiving.

'Will you stay with me? I'm so scared of what's going to happen,' she whispered, and Rosie nodded. There was no way she could go off duty now.

She walked back up the corridor and near the entrance to the Ward located a trolley which she pushed back to Helen's bed. She packed up all of her belongings into a plastic sack that she placed underneath the trolley, and then she helped her patient onto it, locking the side rails in place so there was no risk of falling. She had become adept at manoeuvring trollies with patients on them during her student days, as it was a daily occurrence. A few minutes later she was outside the lift doors, waiting for its arrival. Seconds later, the lift doors opened. A young man and an older woman, presumably his mother, moved aside so she could push the trolley in. As the doors closed behind them and the lift began its descent, they couldn't help sharing their good news with Rosie.

'We're so excited. We've got a beautiful baby boy,' said the woman, holding blue balloons on a string. The excited father joined in the conversation, extolling the virtues of his new son, oblivious to the pain it caused to the silent woman on the trolley.

'I'm off to the pub to wet the baby's head and to buy him his first Stoke City shirt,' he announced, and

Rosie smiled at both of them and wished them both well, as, thankfully, the lift doors opened on each side, allowing visitors to access the way out and Rosie to enter the corridor that took her through Progress and round the corner to the Ward.

The Labour Ward was at its busiest, as inductions from two antenatal floors were now mostly in established labour and had been sent down from the floors above. There were admissions from home of women who had spontaneous labours, as well as women who had high-risk pregnancies because of medical or obstetric problems who were being 'specialled', with one-to-one care in a single side-room. Theatre was in full swing as a planned section for the afternoon had been put back to cope with an emergency that had come in from the community mid-afternoon.

Looking at the notice board on the entrance to the Labour Ward, Rosie saw that Room Four had been allocated for her patient and she expertly manoeuvred her trolley down a corridor that had oxygen cylinders, portable trolleys, spare Perspex babies' cots on wheels and drip stands lining the walls, all waiting to be used as and when required. Anita, one of the Labour Ward auxiliaries, motherly, caring and one of the hardest workers Rosie knew, had just finished mopping the floor as the cleaners were overrun with work. Every Labour Ward bed was now occupied.

'Hey, Rosie, we're ready for you now. I'll give you a hand,' and looking sympathetically at Helen, she helped to manoeuvre the trolley next to the labour bed and helped Helen to slide across onto it.

'You sort your lady out, I'll get rid of the trolley. I'll let the late shift co-ordinator know you have both arrived,' and with that she disappeared back up the corridor.

Helen had retreated into her silent, non-communicative mood, and Rosie's heart went out to her. She was not very experienced in dealing with a labour where the baby had died. She had assisted other more senior Midwives during her training, but being in charge felt very, very different. She was relieved to know that she would be receiving regular support visits from an experienced Midwife working in the room next door and who would be present for the birth if she felt she needed it.

The most difficult part was going to be managing her own emotions, but also being emotionally available for Helen throughout the next few hours. As a newly qualified Midwife, she would be assisted and supported as and when she needed it, part of consolidating her knowledge base into practice, a level of support that would be ongoing throughout her professional working life. She was working additional hours to support Helen, and the Labour Ward co-ordinator was extremely grateful for the extra pair of hands but she was also aware that the young Midwife had been on duty since 7.30 that morning and would probably not be leaving for at least another two or three hours.

Two hours later Helen was nearing delivery. Rosie knew the signs well, and Anita, who was going to be assisting her, was opening up a delivery pack. Helen had finally asked questions about what was going to happen and Rosie had sat on the side of her bed, held her hand and talked her through the next hour. Helen's husband was sitting in the waiting-room, as he had made no decision as to what part of his baby's birth he wanted to be involved in; he was just too distressed.

The baby was only twenty-eight weeks' gestation and would be quite small, probably just two pounds in weight. The second stage of labour would involve less exertion and usually be of short duration, once full dilatation was reached.

Rosie stood by Helen's side, dressed in her green sterile gown, with face-mask and gloves, watching quietly as Helen obeyed and did what her body was telling her to. She could feel some pressure in her bottom and obeyed Rosie's instructions to push. Anita stood at the other side of the bed, holding Helen's hand and whispering quiet words of encouragement. There was a sudden gush of fluid, and slowly and gently, a tiny baby slithered out of the only place where life had been possible for the briefest of time. It was a perfect baby girl, fingers curled into little fists, dark wisps of hair, eyelids still sealed shut. Rosie quickly clamped and cut her cord and then wrapped her in the towel that Anita had passed her.

'Would you like to hold her?' asked Rosie.

There was silence and Rosie waited, patiently, understanding.

'Does she look…?'

'She's just beautiful, and perfectly formed.'

Helen took a great, shuddering breath in, and silently held out her arms. Rosie lifted up the tiny form and placed her gently into her mother's arms. All the love she wanted to give and couldn't almost sliced her in two. The unacknowledged grief that twisted like a knife came gushing out, unstoppable. Tears streamed down Helen's face, while Rosie and Anita waited for the first of many outbursts to slowly abate.

Finally, after some minutes had passed, Helen steeled herself to look. She gazed at the little face that she had tried so hard not to acknowledge as it hurt too much, and used a finger to touch the cheek of her daughter. She gently explored the shape of her face, encouraged by Rosie. Still crying quietly, she no longer feared what she might see, and she pushed the towel covering aside and examined the rest of her baby, laying a gentle hand on the still form of her little one.

Rosie continued her observations and her care, and waited for signs that the placenta had separated as Helen hugged the tiny, still form closer to her chest. She delivered the third stage of labour and noticed that the placenta was quite small and didn't look very healthy; maybe the reason it had not been able to support the life of the baby she had just delivered. She swabbed Helen's birth canal and put a clean sheet under the lower half of her body.

'Shall I go and see your husband and ask him if he wants to come in?' Rosie enquired. Helen nodded and Rosie walked round to the sitting-room in the Progress Department. Helen's husband, Steve, was sitting alone with his head in his hands. He looked up enquiringly. Rosie went and sat next to him.

'You have a daughter. Would you like to come and

meet her? Helen's nursing her at the moment,' she said quietly.

He looked exhausted. Rosie thought he hadn't heard her, or was not going to acknowledge her presence, as he showed no sign that she was there. She realised later that he was just gathering his reserves to do what he knew he must. He sat quietly for a few minutes and then said 'This is the only time I will ever be able to see her,' and he stood up and followed Rosie back to the labour room.

She opened the door and held it for him as he slowly entered. He burst into tears as he approached his wife and daughter, and they embraced, the tiny still form encased between them in her delivery towel. Rosie and Anita quietly attended to tidying up work surfaces around them, trying to give them a little privacy, as they both tried to hide their own tears from the grieving parents.

Helen's tears abated briefly, and then it was she who was showing her daughter to her father, gently opening up the towel to show him how perfect she was, even in death. Rosie ordered some tea for both of them and tucked baby back into her towel and placed her in the cot next to mum's bedside so she could see her whilst she drank her tea.

She answered lots of questions that were now freely asked, about options for commemorating their baby. Rosie knew that whatever she told them now would have to be repeated as the grief and shock of the moment would wipe most of the information away. She told them about the pack of information that would be given to them later, that they could examine in private with time to discuss it with each other and their families.

'Do you have a name for her?' asked Rosie.

Both parents looked at each other.

'Emily, after my mother,' said Helen, 'and Rose, after you.'

Rosie could hardly breathe, let alone speak, she felt so overcome

'I'm honoured that you have given her my name, and I will never forget her,' and she left the room as quickly as she could before her tears blurred her vision. She stood outside the labour room door, drying her eyes and drawing in a few deep breaths to regain control of her emotions before returning to the room and telling both parents to take as much time as they needed to hold and nurse their baby.

Anita had cleared the trolley away and Rosie was busy with her record keeping. Baby Emily was just over twenty-eight weeks, and had not drawn a breath or shown any signs of life at birth. She would be registered as a stillbirth. By the time post-delivery observations and record keeping were completed, and both parents had sat with baby Emily, nursing her for almost two hours, they felt ready to hand her over to staff who would transport her to the hospital mortuary until funeral arrangements could be made. Helen had hugged Rosie fiercely before she was helped onto a trolley and transported up to one of the three postnatal floors.'Thank you,' she said. 'I will never forget you.'

And Rosie's first day as a Staff Midwife was one that she, too, would never forget.

Chapter Nine

Penny was on an early shift and she enjoyed the early drive to the hospital. The sun was out, the birds were singing and all was well with the world. She joined the throng of staff who were all headed in the same direction – the maternity unit. She was really looking forward to her shift that morning as a lady who was pregnant with triplets was being delivered by Caesarean section and she would be warded on the postnatal floor that Penny was working on. She knew the lady in question because for a few weeks she had helped to look after her when, as a student, she was working on the antenatal floors.

She joined her colleagues in the changing rooms where the usual banter and bonhomie was flowing freely. She opened her locker and started to get changed into her uniform which still felt unfamiliar. There was a burst of laughter coming from the next row of lockers and she recognised a couple of the voices and peeped around the corner to see what they were laughing at. One of the student Midwives was holding a hefty piece of sculpture in her hands and when Penny looked closer, she saw that it was the lower half of a male torso with a very pronounced bottom!

She laughed and said, 'Going into the world of antiquities, are we then?' as the student held up the bronze-like piece for the other onlookers to see more closely.

'It's my husband,' she said. 'He's a potter and sculptor and he's doing a series on bottoms, all of them different and I've brought this one in to see if anybody's interested.'

'Reminds me of the bottom of that new Registrar who's just started on the Labour Ward,' somebody said and there were gales of laughter, with a 'and how do YOU know?', followed by more ribbing.

Penny fastened her starched white apron onto her uniform dress and adjusted the equally starched cap onto her short, blonde bob-hair-style, which she pushed out of the way behind each ear. She made sure she'd taken her earrings off as the eagle-eyed Sister Frenchit had told her off in the lift a few days ago when she had forgotten. She was mortified as there were visitors in the lift who smirked and tried to keep a straight face as Sister Frenchit launched into a verbal castigation.

Penny entered the postnatal floor and joined the rest of the staff coming on duty on the early shift. They all gathered in the Sister's office, and stood, catching up with gossip, waiting for the night Sister to give them her report on last night's activities. The night Sister in question was Effie Harrison. She had worked night shifts for years and everybody knew her. She was plump with a large bosom, an ill-defined waist and bunions that she continually complained about to anyone who would listen. She was a kindly soul and looked undressed if she didn't have at least one baby planted firmly on her chest as she multitasked with some other job on the Ward.

A few minutes passed by and she still hadn't appeared, which was almost unheard of. One of the nursery nurses went to look for her, and came back almost immediately, laughing so much she had tears in her eyes. They all looked on in amazement as she doubled up again.

'What's going on?' said Penny, but before she could answer, Effie Harrison appeared behind her.

'Come on. Admit it. Who did it?!'

Her speech was unclear and many words were

muffled. Penny suddenly realised that she didn't have her false teeth in.

'I know one of you did it, you sods. Come on, own up!'

There was a stunned silence, broken by poorly suppressed sniggers, which eventually could not be held back. Effie went on to explain that her poorly fitting false teeth, often very uncomfortable, were stored in water in her denture box in the milk kitchen, where there were two huge fridge freezers. Someone, she glared around her, had put them in the freezer and they were now sitting encased in ice.

She sat down at her desk with the Cardex in front of her with a vexed huff and, muttering under her breath, gathered her thought to the job in hand. Trying to succinctly recount details on twenty-eight mothers and babies, with most of the detail shrouded in technical terminology, and with no teeth in, was a sight to behold. Yet the good-natured Effie valiantly soldiered on whilst one of the auxiliaries was given the job of defrosting her dentures. It was one of the highlights of the day, but the expected arrival of the triplets later on was going to push the incident of Effie's teeth into second place.

With the report given, and Effie delighted that her

teeth were now firmly back in place, a sense of order returned to the Ward, but there were still waves of laughter reverberating as the staff separated and prepared to start tackling the long list of jobs that ensured the smooth running of a twenty-eight bed Postnatal Ward.

Penny knew that the triplet Caesarean was planned for mid-morning. The mother had actually managed to get to thirty-eight weeks of pregnancy, which was a miracle in itself as multiple pregnancies usually went into premature labour as the uterus reached full size before full term. The babies were estimated to be of a good size. Two of the babies were about five pounds in weight and the other baby about four pounds. If they were delivered in good condition, they would be warded with their mother on the postnatal floor. Triplet pregnancies were quite rare and the mother's pregnancy had stimulated a great deal of interest in the obstetric and media world.

The auxiliaries on the Ward started the bed-making round, and the nursery nurses prepared to show new mums how to bathe their babies, make up feeds and how to fold and put on a nappy. Three normal deliveries had been admitted overnight and the routine checks on the mothers' clinical observations needed to be carried out. A number of mothers were due to be discharged home and two other Caesarean births needed bed bathing and help with breast-feeding as they still had intravenous drips in situ.

Penny had just bleeped the Paediatrician who was on call. He was due to arrive shortly to examine a baby who had become very jaundiced. To the uninitiated, the baby looked like he had a healthy suntan, but his condition was causing some concern. Many healthy new-borns became slightly jaundiced after birth as part of the process of adjusting physiologically to a life outside the uterus. During their intrauterine life, babies had lots of extra red blood cells needed to keep them well-oxygenated during their stay inside their mother's body. After birth, when the excess red blood cells were no longer needed, they were broken down in the baby's body and then eliminated.

One of the waste products was a substance called bilirubin, which stained the skin yellow. If bilirubin levels were high, they could affect the functioning of the baby's brain and cause a condition called kernicterus. Light therapy was used to help break down the levels of bilirubin in the skin tissues and babies would be nursed naked in their cots, with large eye pads secured around their face to protect them from discomfort.

Penny went into the nursery at the end of the Ward to check on her little patient. He was fast asleep, limbs splayed out, and quite comfortable. Overhead cot heaters and the warmth generated by the light ensured that a baby's body temperature did not drop below normal. Most of the babies from this side of the Ward were still in the nursery as they were removed from their mother's side during the night to give their mothers an opportunity to sleep. The night staff had the job of feeding them all, those that were bottle-feeding. It was quite a task, as up to twenty babies may have needed to be fed, alongside all other duties, and usually there would be just one Midwife and one auxiliary or nursery nurse on duty at night.

The Perspex cots on wheels that allowed all-round vision were lined up in regimented rows with their occupants wrapped in sheets and either a blue or a pink blanket, denoting the sex of the infant. There was a precise way of folding the swaddling sheets that most staff seemed to adhere to. Even the outer blanket cover was arranged and manipulated into an envelope-type fold at the bottom. The nursery was a lovely place to be in. It was warm, brightly lit, with big open windows that let in a lot of light. There were comfy armchairs for mothers who were breast-feeding to sit in, and a radio playing music in the background created a homely feel. Frequently, there were parents being shown how to bathe their babies, nervously balancing them on their knee as member of staff gave them instructions.

Sister Carter was the sister in charge of the Postnatal Ward that morning. A seasoned veteran, there wasn't much she hadn't seen or experienced throughout her many years of Midwifery practice. Her navy-blue-clad figure could be seen instructing her troops in a brisk, no-nonsense attitude. She ran her Ward with a practised ease which, to junior staff, she made look effortless. She had used to work in what was called 'the old block' – a building about three hundred yards away from the building she was working in now. It was old, dilapidated and had stood for a hundred years or more. Facilities were terribly out-dated and not fit for purpose, which had resulted in the new maternity unit being built and opened in 1968. If delivery rooms were full in the old building, women had to deliver on wooden bath boards, literally! It was archaic beyond belief and the move into the six-floor maternity unit was readily welcomed by all staff.

Sister Carter was trying to juggle with the usual problem of who was ready to go home and was fit for discharge. The number of beds needed for newly delivered mothers, based on the Labour Ward's deliveries that morning, was difficult to estimate at the best of times. She knew that by teatime the inductions from that morning would all be nearing delivery and would be needing a bed somewhere. It was a bit like balancing the books in financial terms, except the currency wasn't cash it was mothers and babies! From the daybook that sat on the desk at the Midwife station on the centre of the Ward, she could see at a glance each room on the Ward, with the number of beds in each and the name of each patient, giving her a very good grasp of the workload. Mothers who had experienced a normal delivery usually had a hospital stay of five days, or more if the Midwife thought they needed extra support. Caesarean births did not get discharged home until the tenth day. Forceps deliveries were discharged around the seventh day.

As Sister Carter was grappling with the daily intricacies of bed management, Penny was still in the nursery, enjoying settling down a baby who was crying. She nursed her little charge until the crying stopped and then tucked her back into her cot. As she stood back from the cot, she glanced up at the back row of cots, giving a last confirmation that all was well. She froze momentarily then slammed her hand onto the emergency buzzer which was on the wall where she was standing. The noise was shocking in its intensity.

The baby she had glimpsed in the cot near to the back wall of the nursery was deeply cyanosed. She could see it clearly, even from the distance from where she was standing. The ear-piercing shriek of the emergency buzzer reverberated throughout the Ward and beyond, calling to arms anyone and everyone. The flashing light, located above the door to the nursery, indicated where the emergency was. Penny acted quickly. She frantically pushed other cots aside in her haste to get to the distressed baby and as she reached the cot Sister Carter burst through the door.

'He's not breathing.'

'Bring him over here,' and Sister Carter yanked a wall-mounted oxygen supply tube and tiny face mask together and placed a baby change mat onto the Resuscitaire. Penny was shaking as she placed the limp, unresponsive form onto the mat. She had seen a number of babies in varying degrees of respiratory distress, but none of them had looked as severe as this.

By this time, another staff Midwife, an auxiliary and a nursery nurse had almost collided as they all reached the door of the nursery together.

'Go and get me a Paediatrician now,' instructed

Sister Carter, and the auxiliary ran back down the Ward to use the telephone. Sister Carter placed the face mask over the baby's nose and mouth and turned the oxygen supply on at the wall. The baby's skin was almost grey and his little limbs were floppy as he was placed onto the infant Resuscitaire. Sister Carter could see there was no respiratory effort – the baby's chest was not moving. She placed a finger on the delicate, thin skin over the infant's heart. Nothing. She inserted the ear pieces of her stethoscope and placed the round, metal disc onto the baby's chest and listened. A minute passed by in complete silence. Penny was inwardly praying that the oxygen would enable the baby's failing respiratory system to kick-start into action again. It didn't.

Midwives were not in their training given instruction in the use of laryngoscopes or how to carry out advanced resuscitation procedures, but Sister Carter however, had, in a previous role, worked for many years in a neonatal unit. She had also worked in her professional capacity in Third World countries and Save the Children agencies. She was one of the very few Midwives who had received intensive training and was competent at using a range of advanced resuscitation skills.

'Get me a laryngoscope and tube out of the drawer.'

This to Penny, who did as she was asked. She opened up the laryngoscope from its sterile pack and handed it to Sister Carter who by this time had removed the baby's cotton top so she could observe his chest more easily. She gently tipped the baby's head back and, taking the laryngoscope, she inserted the stainless-steel blade down the back of baby's throat to access the airway and its link to baby's lungs. It had been two-and-a-half minutes since she had arrived, and she didn't know how long the baby had been in respiratory distress before her arrival.

'Where the hell is that Paediatrician?' she said to no one in particular, as she prepared to slide a tiny tube down the laryngoscope into baby's lungs, which in turn would be attached to the oxygen supply.

Her prayers were answered almost immediately as more running footsteps preluded the arrival of the on-call Paediatrician who fortunately had been on his way to the Ward to carry out some check-ups on babies he had arranged to see. Penny had never been so glad to see anyone in her life and felt like hugging him. She breathed a huge sigh of relief as the Paediatrician took over and within seconds had a life-saving supply of oxygen being pumped directly to baby's lungs. Another nail-biting minute passed before any sign of improvement could be seen: some erratic movements of baby's chest wall, a change in the terrible, grey pallor of baby's skin, a lessening of the deep blue cyanosis, a slow return to dusky and then, finally, pink. An attempted cry signalled the removal of the tube and laryngoscope.

Baby started to cry and the face mask oxygen supply was continued for a few minutes longer until the Paediatrician was happy with the baby's condition.

Sister Carter returned to her management of the Ward and left Penny assisting the Paediatrician. Her first job, as the Paediatrician carried out a top to toe assessment of the baby, was to go and find the baby's mother who, throughout the drama of the last half an hour, had been in one of the Ward's bathrooms, having no knowledge of the near disaster that had threatened her baby's life. She had had a traumatic forceps delivery in the middle of the night and little sleep and had been looking forward to her first bath, hoping it would help soothe her battered perineum that had three layers of stitches holding it together. She paled visibly and almost stumbled out of the bath in her haste to get to her baby when Penny gently explained what had happened. Penny then helped her to dry and put on a clean nightgown, reassuring her that the Paediatrician was still with her baby and that he would then come and see her.

He spent some time talking to the baby's mother about what had happened. He reassured her that baby's condition was now fine, but he was going to order a number of tests as a precautionary measure to find out what had caused her baby to become so compromised. After more reassurance, baby was wheeled back to the side of his mother's bed and Penny headed for the desk area where she proceeded to order a chest X-ray and to arrange for swabs to be taken to detect any signs of infection. She updated Sister Carter on the Paediatrician's instructions and then went to immerse herself into the much more calming job of helping to fix a reluctant baby onto her mother's breast.

At 11.30, Sister Carter received the news that the triplets had been delivered safely by Caesarean section, were all in good condition and would shortly be arriving onto her Ward. A side room had already been prepared for mum and three sets of baby clothes – tie-at-the-back cotton nightgowns and knitted bonnets and bootees, providing extra warmth for the smaller, less mature babies – were all set out in the nursery waiting to be wrapped around the extra special new arrivals.

Twenty minutes later, the doors to the Ward were opened by Sid the Porter and two nursery nurses, pushing and pulling three cots between them like a wagon-train in a cowboy movie, one behind the other. Most mums returned to the Ward with their baby being pushed in a wheelchair, and this unusual arrival in every sense of the word created delight and interest from everyone right down to the cleaners, milk-room staff and family members awaiting news of their wives' discharge who were sitting in the waiting-room. There were lots of 'ooos' and 'aahs' as the babies, of which two were identical, were pushed into one of the nurseries. Their mother would be joining them later after she had recovered from her surgery.

Lunch time arrived in a blink of an eye. The Ward had been busy with routine tasks, admissions, discharges, the Paediatrician's round, the doctor's round, and the arrival of the lovely ladies who came to visit all newborns and tested their hearing with special equipment. Mothers who were not well enough to get out of bed needed bed bathing and their babies also needed their first bath if just delivered. The late shift staff would soon be arriving, who would need to be updated on the morning's events, and the lunch trolleys containing hot food, cooked on site were also scheduled to be delivered to the ward. Any mobile patients would all gather in the day room to be served their midday meal. Just the hustle and bustle of a normal day's activities on a busy postnatal floor that was being re-enacted in every maternity unit across the length and breadth of the British Isles.

After her lunch break, Penny was busy examining mothers, making sure their postnatal observations were within normal limits. She checked that the mothers' uteri were involuting, slowly shrinking back to their pre-pregnant size. These abdominal examinations also included a check to see if any perineal stitches were healing and that no infection was developing. She hurried to finish her tasks so she could spend a little extra time with her next patient. The latter was three days old and her fifteen-year-old mother had been discharged home the day after she delivered. Baby Charlotte was to be adopted and would soon be handed over into the care of Social Services.

Penny, and the other staff on the Ward, made a big effort to spend time with her, hold and nurse her as much as possible so she didn't miss out on the crucial skin-to-skin contact that a newborn needs as much as it needs milk. It was so sad, thought Penny, that a baby couldn't stay with its birth mother. It was a difficult situation for the young woman; her family was unsupportive and she had no means to support herself. In the early 1970s, it was not uncommon to see babies that were to be adopted housed on the Postnatal Wards for up to a week.

Charlotte was getting ready for her feed, becoming restless and mouthing at the sheet wrapped around her when her mouth came into contact with it. Penny stroked her pink, velvety cheek and her finger was immediately taken by the little rosebud mouth.

'OK, little one, it's coming.'

Penny had already prepared what she needed by obtaining a bottle of feed from the big fridge in the milk kitchen. The feeds were made up in bulk, downstairs in the basement area of the hospital, and each ward had a daily delivery. She warmed the feed up by standing the feeding bottle in a jug of hot water for a few minutes and then settled herself down in one of the armchairs that were scattered around the nursery.

The only sounds that could be heard for the next twenty minutes were contented sucking and murmuring noises as baby Charlotte tucked into her bottle feed with gusto. She was a good little feeder and finished her bottle with a resounding burp when Penny tucked her, upright, into her shoulder. She was already asleep, sated and full of milk, by the time Penny had finished changing her nappy and she tucked her back into her cot.

Closing the nursery door behind her she walked back up the corridor and almost bumped into the Paediatrician whom she had assisted with the emergency at the beginning of the shift. He had the results of the tests carried out on baby that morning. Penny called for Sister Carter and they went into the office where there was an X-ray viewing light on the wall. He turned the viewer on and pushed the film into it.

They all peered closely at the illuminated X-ray.

'He has a hole between the right and left ventricles of the heart that didn't close at birth as it should have. So, there's a lot less oxygenated blood being pumped out around baby's body, hence the cyanosis attack. Baby will need to be monitored on Special Care Baby Unit but first I need to speak to the parents. Can you ring SCBU and let them know we will need a cot? I've already talked to the Consultant Paediatrician on call.'

'I'll come with you to see Mum,' said Sister Carter. 'She's going to be really upset; she still hasn't recovered from the shock of this morning, poor soul, and now this.'

Sister Carter followed the Paediatrician to the room where a mother was to receive some news that would turn her and her husband's life upside down for the foreseeable future.

The findings on the X-ray had never been seen by Penny before but she had heard of the heart condition. A baby, growing inside the womb, had a different blood circulation through the heart as blood did not need to be pumped to the inactive lungs for oxygenation. The mother's body provided oxygen via the cord blood vessels, and a small opening allowed blood to pass between the two bottom chambers of the heart whilst the baby was still in utero. When the baby was born and took that first great breath in, changes in pressure within the heart closed the small opening, and with the cutting of the cord, the foetal circulation was closed down.

Occasionally, the small opening between the bottom two chambers of the heart did not close and seal properly, as it was in this baby's case.

'Midwifery is such a world of extremes,' mused Penny, as she gathered her cloak and bag from the store cupboard on the corridor. One young mother forced through life's circumstances into leaving her baby behind, another mother, who had a much-loved and wanted baby that came close to dying that morning, desperate for her baby to cling onto life at any cost, and downstairs on the antenatal floors women in difficult social circumstances having terminations, allowable up to twenty-eight weeks of pregnancy, because they just didn't want another baby. 'There's no rhyme or reason to it,' she thought. And trying to push aside the seeming unfairness of it all, and failing, she left the Ward in the competent hands of the late shift staff.

Chapter Ten

'It's going to be a busy one,' said Rosie. She was standing with Sylvia at the small kiosk situated in the antenatal clinic, where the WVS volunteer ladies provided hot drinks and sold snacks to patients and staff alike. A few months had passed by so very quickly as they got to grips with working on their allocated ward areas. There was, they rapidly discovered, still so much to learn. Regular updating lecture days were provided for all staff, based in the large classroom which was sited over the antenatal clinic, where they had, as students, almost lived for the past two years. They had both just spent an hour being updated about the new Syntocinon regimes that three different Consultants wanted to be administered to their patients. They all wanted a slightly different prescription of the drug that would slowly be dripped intravenously into their patients' arms to help trigger labour.

'Why they can't all decide to use the same one, I don't know,' moaned Sylvia. 'There's very little difference between the doses anyway.'

They threaded their way through the crowds of pregnant women who were queuing at the reception desk of the antenatal clinic, waiting to be sent through to the various sections of that department where blood tests, X-rays, and scans were carried out.

'I'm sure there must be a baby boom going on – I've never seen it as packed as this,' said Rosie.

'I know what it is,' said Sylvia, and Rosie looked at her.

'What?'

'It's almost nine months since last Christmas!' and they both laughed.

Sylvia's summing up was probably quite accurate. Regularly as clockwork, every year in September, many more babies that month would be born. The same situation occurred nine months after Bank Holidays or extra special events, like a royal occasion or winning a national football event, when choices for babies' names would be made from the members of the football team. The mating rituals of the human race would have provided a thought-provoking dissertation for anyone brave enough to take on its myriads of complexity, but the two young Midwives had more urgent matters in mind.

They purchased chocolate bars and snacks to fortify themselves against the inevitable missed lunch breaks and returned to their prospective ward areas, planning to meet up if they were lucky enough to have been allocated a lunch break later.

A new set of student Midwives had been allocated to the Labour Ward and Sylvia, along with every other qualified Midwife, would be assigned one to take under her wing. It was rare for a Midwife to be without a student of some sort or other by her side. Not only did Midwives support student Midwives, but also new medical students and student nurses, who, as part of their training, were required to have three months of obstetric experience. If staff ratios were low, sometimes they had two students in tow to teach, monitor, advise and support as they looked after their patients.

Sylvia had been allocated a new student called Stella Steel. She enjoyed the enthusiasm and hard-working students she had been supporting so far, and loved seeing them blossom with a bit of praise and encouragement. It was only a short time ago that she herself had been standing in their shoes. She hung her cloak up in the Midwives' sitting-room and joined the rest of the staff for the handover of care from the night shift. Amazingly, there were three empty labour rooms which, Sylvia knew, wouldn't last for long. It gave her a good opportunity to spend a bit of extra time with the new student.

Stella Steel stood at the back of the small group of students who were being shown the layout of the Labour Ward and where everything was, prior to meeting the Midwife she would be with during her time on the Labour Ward … and she was bored already.

When she had applied for training as a direct entrant, with no previous nursing experience, she had envisaged the exciting world of handsome doctors, and the status of deference and admiration bestowed upon the smart, navy-clad nurses, just like she had viewed on TV programmes such as Emergency Ward Ten. She saw her training as an inescapable route that she must travel down to gain some of that prestige in her life.

A dreary existence of working in dusty, dirty pot banks that littered the skyline of where she lived held no interest for her.

In her late twenties, training to become a professional woman was a means to an end, nothing more. She wasn't drawn to entering the caring profession, as it was called. She actually didn't like babies that much, but when searching for some means to support herself, she had seen that they were recruiting for Midwifery students and, compared to what else was on offer, it seemed like the best of a bad bunch, so she had applied.

One of the attributes that gave her some leeway was the fact that she had a photographic memory, which would come in very useful. She could retain information quite easily without necessarily understanding it. Her own self-interest scored highly on any chart outlining her objectives in life, and being able to churn out easily remembered facts and figures, even if she didn't understand them, was the easier route to get to where she wanted.

The group of students in her set had already annoyed her intensely. They were young, noisy, soppy and sweet to the point of being nauseous.

They actually oohed and aahed over babies and almost fell over themselves to please anybody who requested anything. They reminded her a bit of her younger sister who had come top in the class at everything she ever attempted. Not that Stella wasn't academically capable, she was, but she had no interest in flogging herself to death to achieve what she thought the world owed her. The entrance exam wasn't that difficult and, besides, there were ways and means of getting around that obstacle.

Her unmissable 'I'm better than you lot' demeanour and lack of interest in anybody but herself had made her few, if any, friends, but that didn't worry her in the slightest; she wasn't there to make friends. And so, crossing her arms, and switching off from the barrage of information that was being given to her from the Midwife explaining the layout of the Labour Ward, she yawned and tried to feign an interest she didn't feel.

Sylvia had discovered that one of the best ways of finding her way around the many rooms and storage areas of the Labour Ward was to have to stock up on all the supplies that each room needed. It didn't take long to become familiar with what was needed where, as the continual checking of each cupboard, drawer, and piece of equipment soon embedded the seemingly unimportant task of where to go to get a laryngoscope in a hurry if the one in use failed to function. Often, a terse instruction to get something quickly was because an emergency was taking place, involving the life of a mother or a baby. It was essential therefore that all staff knew exactly where the clinical tools of their trade could be found.

And so it was that this task, along with the no-touch technique of putting on a pair of sterile gloves without contaminating them, was on the agenda for

Stella Steel on her first day on the Ward. Sylvia had introduced herself and told her what the morning's activities were going to be. Stacking shelves and putting on gloves, Stella decided, were not the activities that she thought would be a priority for herself. Surely the cleaners or auxiliaries did that.

She hated Sister Frenchit on sight, who was assigned to showing them how to open a packet of gloves, for God's sake. When she had marshalled them like children into a room and lined them up, her first thought was 'Who's this bullying old bird?' Sister Frenchit's eyes, like lasers, had landed on her, resulting in a curt command of 'My name is Sister Frenchit – nothing more, nothing less. I don't like slang terms, answering back and any talking during my teaching sessions. Is that clear?' And the whole group of students, in unison, like a class of four-year-olds, had responded, 'Yes, Sister Frenchit.' Stella was canny enough to recognise that in Sister Frenchit she may have met her match and decided she was definitely someone to be wary of in the future.

'This is going to be a long day,' thought Stella, as she failed for the third time the objective of putting on a pair of sterile rubber gloves without contaminating the outsides.

Sylvia found the new student an anomaly. She didn't talk much, asked few questions, and didn't have the same eager, interested demeanour that every other student she had worked with had, in abundance. At first, she thought it was just a front for shyness and a lack of self-confidence, and remembering her first days on the Labour Ward, she wasn't too worried. Each student had their own time frame for settling in and getting to grips with the barrage of information that they had to assimilate from the moment they started their training. But now, she wasn't so sure.

Beryl, who worked as an auxiliary in theatre, had crossed swords with Stella during her first week working on the Ward. Stella had been rostered to go into theatre to observe a Caesarean Section. She knew she could not enter the theatre directly, and must enter through the female staff changing rooms. There, she would change into theatre scrubs and white wellingtons before proceeding through to another area inside the theatre itself where a long row of stainless sinks allowed staff to scrub up before donning theatre gowns, masks and gloves. She was fifteen minutes late and staff were already inside the scrub-up area. She changed into bottle green scrubs, put on a disposable mask and stepped into the theatre area which was crowded with staff as the Caesarean section was for a twin pregnancy.

There were trolleys of instruments everywhere and Stella could see that the patient was now anaesthetised and being transferred across onto a central stainless-steel table. She saw a sterile pack of a green theatre gown on top of a trolley and surreptitiously grabbed it off the top, hoping no one would see her. She hadn't noticed Beryl behind her who, with reflexes that an Olympian would admire, slapped at her fingers as she reached and touched the top of the trolley in her attempt to grab the theatre gown. Unfortunately Beryl was just too late to stop the contact of Stella's unwashed, non-sterile hands on the sterile trolley which was loaded with instruments.

Beryl's involuntary 'No! Don't touch that,' was a microsecond too late. Heads turned as an exasperated Beryl said, 'You've contaminated the trolley with unwashed hands and no gloves: it will have to be dismantled and set up again with more instruments!'

Stella just shrugged and said, 'Well, it was the only gown I could see and I couldn't come in without one.'

She wasn't embarrassed at all that she had delayed the start of the Caesarean section by another ten minutes, which, if it had been an emergency, could have had dire consequences. An hour later, as she was leaving theatre, Beryl noticed that Stella had not changed into theatre wellies, either, and still had on her black, lace-up shoes. Beryl tackled her about it; a reprimand that barely dented Stella's view of 'petty rules'.

Over the next few weeks, Sylvia became more and more concerned about Stella. Give her something to read and recite, and then recall, she was word perfect. Ask her to apply the knowledge to practice by using information she had gleaned from examining a patient, she floundered. Consolidating knowledge and practical experience was an absolutely crucial skill for Midwives, a skill that needed to be in use every day of their working life.

Teaching a student to accurately assess the dilatation of a woman's cervix during labour involved meshing together detailed anatomy, physiology, and an interpretation of what her fingers were telling her through the nuances of sensitive touch. On a number of occasions, Stella had been incredibly confident in carrying out internal examinations, using the correct terminology to tell the Midwife what she was feeling. But after checking by the Midwife, she was found to be so far off the mark that Sylvia wondered if she had even found the neck of the womb at all, let alone given an accurate assessment of its dilatation.

Stella wasn't too worried about the number of times Midwives seemed to want to go over tasks with her. She had two years to get it right, and what was it that one of the Consultants had said during lectures the other week, the one with the wry sense of humour?

'There's only one way in and one way out, and basically, that's it.'

Another problem area for Stella's learning was locating and counting the foetal heart rate, a skill that had to be mastered very early on. During examinations of pregnant women, she had vigorously confirmed that yes, she could hear it, through the black, trumpet-like stethoscope that was placed onto a pregnant abdomen, and even voiced, after counting with her fob watch, what the rate per minute was, but Sylvia knew she was faking it.

To be able to ascertain and count the rate of the baby's heartbeat in a minute, the position of how the baby was lying inside the uterus needed to be confirmed with accuracy as either baby's chest or back area was the place, externally, on the mother's abdomen, where the Pinard stethoscope needed to be placed. At Stella's last attempt, she had insisted she could hear the baby's heartbeat low down on the mother's abdomen, with the Pinard placed directly over a baby's bottom, a breech presentation that she also couldn't and hadn't identified.

Students needing extra time and support to master the skills required were not a problem for Sylvia, as she knew all students were different in their abilities. Usually, those who had struggled early on to acquire competencies had, by the end of the first year, become competent and were being signed off in their abdominal palpations register by the assessing Midwife.

The issue that really concerned her was Stella's dogged insistence on a number of occasions that she was right when she most definitely wasn't. There was an occasional success, but Sylvia felt that those results were more by good luck and the law of averages than any skill on the participant's part. Stella found it difficult to receive feedback highlighting areas for improvement, regardless of how professional and supportive the assessing Midwives were. At the most, a very begrudging admittance that she might have got it wrong had to be wrung out of her. As the day progressed and the Labour Ward girded its loins for an unprecedented number of admissions and averted near disasters, Stella Steel perfected the art of being seen to be busy whilst performing the minimum effort possible for the rest of her shift.

Chapter Eleven

When Rosie Smith had been assigned to Sister Frenchit's ward, her heart had sunk. Sister Frenchit had a reputation as a strict authoritarian who ran her ward with military precision. It was a shame she didn't display the personal qualities of empathy and support that would have eased the stress levels of the staff working on her ward, when the going got tough.

As the months of working there passed by, Rosie began to appreciate a little more the superb organisation of layers of protocols, policy and procedures that Sister Frenchit was responsible for. She was still not liked by many mothers and the students were afraid of her, yet she was like a walking, talking Margaret Myles – the great tome of a text book that was obligatory reading for anyone studying Midwifery – and admiring her skill sets made the burden of her unapproachable demeanour a little more bearable.

Rosie was working a late shift and the evening visitors were in. She had the unenviable job of making sure no one had any more than two visitors at a time for the one hour of visiting allocated between eight and nine o'clock. Sister Frenchit regularly instructed the late shift to check each bedside and make sure there were no more than two people visiting behind the drawn curtains. Rosie hated doing it. Some of the patients were in for six or eight weeks at a time, with young children at home and husbands who worked shifts and found it difficult to get to the hospital at all. Anything she could do to ease the burden of separation was justified, and if there was one rule meant to be broken, this was it.

Often, during visiting hours at night, Sister Frenchit would retire to her office, close the door, and not emerge again until visiting hour was at an end. That suited Rosie just fine, as she could conveniently turn a blind eye to the odd extra visitor.

She was sitting quietly at the Midwife station, going through patients' records for the umpteenth time that day, trying to keep up to date with thirty-four diagnoses of the women housed on the Ward, the tests they had had, and what their progress was. It was the first time since 11.30 that morning that she had actually sat down other than for a quick sandwich from the

WVS kiosk on the antenatal clinic. As she sat there, her senses were alerted to a strange smell drifting down from the big, six-bedded ward at the end of the corridor. She couldn't work out what it was, and it was getting stronger. She stood up and walked briskly down the corridor into Room One where the smell seemed to be the strongest.

All of the beds had their curtains drawn around them, giving patients and visitors a little extra privacy. The aroma was much stronger now and was definitely food-related. She approached the bed in the farthest corner next to the window and quietly peeped through the curtain. Mrs Amina Begum, her husband and their two toddlers were tucking into an extensive menu of curry, rice, naan breads and a variety of sauces, spread like a picnic across the NHS logos on the coverlet on the bed. The poor lady had really struggled with the food choices on offer in the hospital. English food was unknown to her as she had only recently arrived in England before she was admitted to the maternity hospital with a raised blood pressure.

Rosie silently withdrew, and tiptoed back out of the room, hoping that if Sister Frenchit kept to her routine, the culinary evidence would have been cleared away before she appeared from her office.

Bang on nine o'clock, the click of Sister Frenchit's office door opening heralded her appearance at the desk where Rosie was sitting. She stood in the middle of the corridor as visitors swarmed around her petite frame, heading for the lifts and stairs as they made their way home.

'Staff Nurse Smith, what's that terrible smell?'

Rosie feigned surprise and puzzlement as she responded with,

'I have no idea, Sister Frenchit. I think it's coming from the Room Twelve end.'

She stood up and tried to steer Sister Frenchit to the other end of the Ward as, out of the corner of her eye, she saw Mr Begum and his two toddlers walking up the corridor clutching a variety of used food cartons to his chest. She managed to get Sister Frenchit past her office door and was relieved to see Mr Begum disappear round the corner to the lifts. The night staff appeared then, and Sister Frenchit was diverted from her mission, and went back into her office to hand over her patients' reports and update on their care.

The next day, in the coffee room in the basement, Rosie was sitting with Penny and Sylvia recounting the previous night's escapade. They were laughing and wondered what Sister Frenchit would have said if she had discovered the misdemeanour! On another table next to them a staff Midwife leaned across and said,

'I can better that one!'

They all turned around to look at her.

'Last year I was on duty with Sister Frenchit when a patient's husband came up to the desk during visiting time and complained of 'noises' in their ward that were upsetting the ladies. "Noises?" said Sister Frenchit. "What do you mean, 'noises'?" The husband just looked sheepish and repeated his claim that there was a problem.

As you can imagine, Sister Frenchit was not best pleased. She stood up, annoyed that her routine had been disturbed and marched down the corridor to confront the culprit who was disturbing her peace. She followed the husband into the four-bedded room, who pointed a finger at a bed, concealed by its closed curtains. She grabbed hold of the curtain and pulled it aside, to be met with the naked, flabby buttocks of the husband of Linda Stuart who occupied the bed and was an inpatient for induction. He had the grace to look embarrassed and tried, unsuccessfully, to cover his rapidly shrinking penis with his hands. His wife stoutly defended their amorous coupling, saying that everybody knew that "if you did it the night before, it could start you off in labour."

"And anyway," she said belligerently, "we were just saving you the job of starting me off.'"

By this time, the whole of the coffee room was in an uproar. Sylvia had tears running down her face, and when she, Penny and Rosie returned to their allocated wards they were still laughing about the intricacies and foibles of human nature.

Chapter Twelve

Elizabeth Montgomery, Head of Midwifery Services, sat at her desk with three letters of complaint in front of her. She ran a hand through her immaculate, coiffured hair and sat back, deep in thought behind the desk that dominated her office.

It was all so unusual. Three women who had delivered at her hospital in the last twelve months, all who spoke little if any English, all complaining that their requests for more pain relief had been ignored by the Midwife caring for them. Never in her thirty-five-year career had she been involved in anything like it. Usually, it was the other way around; lots of lovely letters from grateful patients, extolling the skills and care given by her Midwives.

She had requested the patients' notes as soon as the letters had arrived and read through the records of the women's care, twice. According to the notes, each woman had had at least one dose of Pethidine during their labour and in the other two cases they were given two doses of Pethidine. Here were women claiming they had not been given pain relief in the form of Pethidine and yet in the notes it was written by the Midwife that she had given it. To make matters worse, it was the same Midwife who had looked after the women in labour, a coincidence on a par with winning the 'Pools'. The next anomaly was that the Midwife in question had an excellent reputation; there had been no problems ever reported with her standards of care.

Elizabeth had met with one of the Supervisors of Midwives, whose job it was to support best practice and investigate any claims of sub-standard care. It was routine, every month, to pull at random a dozen set of notes and analyse the standard of care given. If unsound judgement or poor record keeping was picked up, the Midwife in question would be advised, supported, offered updating or extra training and then assessed to ensure fitness for practice had been restored. They had examined the cases and then called the Midwife in to give an account of her care of the three women.

The Midwife being investigated had been deeply distressed when she was informed that there was not only one complaint, but three. She had sobbed and said she couldn't understand it. She had gone through the records with the Supervisor, trying to recall the ladies, but it was difficult with twelve months of other deliveries in between. She rarely gave two doses of Pethidine, she said, but there in the notes was her signature, twice. She had commented that on one occasion she had gone home early, with permission, as her mother was ill, and so she couldn't have been there at the time the second injection of Pethidine was given to the patient, who still insisted that she hadn't been given the second dose anyway. And the red pen used to write in the notes that Pethidine had been given was a slightly different colour from the pens she used, which she brought in batches of six at a time, as she got through so many.

The Supervisor of Midwives had no option but to suspend her from duty until further investigations had taken place. Elizabeth had felt terrible, but one of her prime, overarching objectives was to protect the public by providing the highest standard of Midwifery services possible. The Supervisor of Midwives escorted the still crying Midwife out of her office. Seconds later, she had another visitor.

Elizabeth heard a knock on her door and she called out, 'Come in,' deep in thought. There was something very wrong here, she knew, and was determined to get to the bottom of it. Charles Merton, Consultant Obstetrician, entered, looking immaculate, as usual, and oozing just a little too much charm for Elizabeth's liking.

'Ah, Charles, thanks for coming to see me at such short notice. Have a seat. Would you like some tea?'

'No thanks, I've just come from the Trust's board meeting and I'm awash with the stuff,' and he adjusted his cuffs, unconsciously smoothing his silver grey hair back, and positioning his designer, gold-rimmed glasses onto the end of his nose. He gave Elizabeth one of his best 'aren't I the greatest?' smiles which worked most of the time on the female staff, but not on Elizabeth, and sat down on the easy chair facing her desk.

'What can I do for you?' he asked.

'I'm investigating some complaints about a Midwife's care. It seems some patients didn't get enough pain relief, although the notes say otherwise. I believe that one of these ladies ended up in theatre when you were on call and I wondered if you can remember the case?'

Charles looked at the set of notes that she handed him and he casually flipped through them, frowning in concentration in parts, looking concerned. He looked up and rubbed the side of his nose before sighing.

'Well, quite frankly Elizabeth, no. I remember it was a really busy week around that time and I did a long list of planned sections, but nothing comes to mind. You say they complained about pain relief? Sorry,' and he handed the notes back.

'It's just so odd. There are two signatures here saying she had two doses. The patient says she didn't get two doses of Pethidine, but needed them, and the Midwife says she didn't remember giving two doses, but it's written in red in the notes that she gave them!'

'It sounds to me like you have a Midwife lacking in the professional standards that we demand,' he said, stating the obvious. She's obviously got some record keeping deficits. I presume you are going to take the necessary steps to preclude her from practice until you sort this out. We really don't need Midwives of this calibre, especially on the Labour Ward.' He looked pointedly at his gold Omega watch and stood up.

'Sorry, must dash. I have some room patients waiting to see me on Ward Fifty-Four. Mustn't keep Sister Frenchit waiting, must we?'

And with that he left quickly, shutting the door quietly behind him.

In the corridor outside Elizabeth's door he took a

deep shuddering breath and tried to calm himself down. He knew exactly who the patient was – she had ended up as a section for failure to progress and maternal distress, caused by his greater need for the Pethidine than she. He hadn't counted on patients complaining, especially those uneducated ethnics who spoke no English. He thought he was onto a safe bet there. The problem was that, as his addiction progressed, after the first couple of hours of euphoria following his fix, he became so drowsy and inattentive that he had difficulty in concentrating, even for short periods. He couldn't afford to make any mistakes.

He knew the forged signature was a pretty good replica and they couldn't prove anything. He knew he would have to be extra careful in future, because the one unchangeable factor was that he couldn't function without a regular supply of Pethidine. He wiped the sweat off his brow with his handkerchief and tried to ignore the very fine tremor that was developing in his hands as he headed at a brisk walk to the lift that would take him to that bitch of a Midwife who was in charge of the Antenatal Ward.

Elizabeth stayed at her desk for another half an hour after Charles Merton had left and scrutinised the notes yet again. She ruminated on the meeting that had just taken place. Although the quality of Charles

Merton's work was definitely not in any question, she just didn't like him. He courted, no, needed adulation, evidenced by the posse of acolytes always hanging around him. He had many areas of expertise, was brilliant at public speaking and his skills in theatre were legendary. He had quite a name, nationally, but there was just something she didn't like about him that she couldn't put her finger on. Sighing, she gathered the notes up in her arms, left her office and went to speak to the Number Seven who had overall responsibility of the Labour Ward.

Sylvia was busy, helping Beryl to clean and replenish used stock in the labour room where she had just delivered a baby. As usual, the Ward was bursting at the seams, with an atmosphere akin to that of a busy railway station. That earlier sense of being overwhelmed by the responsibility of the level of care she was giving was slowly being replaced by an inner core of deep satisfaction. She still got attacks of 'the Collywobbles' as her mother called them, moments of panic and anxiety as she experienced clinical abnormalities that she had only read about during her training.

Last week was a typical example. Another Midwife had delivered a baby whose deformities were so severe they were incompatible with life. A seemingly uneventful pregnancy, a short, uneventful labour, followed by a normal delivery. Except that the baby had numerous abnormalities. Sylvia was grateful that she had an opportunity to see the effects that nature sometimes cruelly inflicted on babies and their families, hoping that when she too was faced with the stress of handling such a tragic situation, she would have strength enough for both herself as well as her patient.

There was nothing in her training that could have helped any Midwife to adequately cope with the shock of recognising an undiagnosed gross abnormality, inflicted upon a baby she had just delivered, sometimes crying and alive, and knowing that in seconds, her patient's first words to her would be 'Is he alright?'

Frequently, discussions took place at higher levels about the need for a counsellor who would be there to support Midwives who themselves became traumatised by some of the cases they had to deal with, but nothing ever materialised. Midwives had to carry on supporting each other emotionally, when the going got really tough, which it did with an alarming regularity.

Down in the basement Stella Steel was changing into her uniform and getting ready to start on a late shift. She was working on Sister Frenchit's antenatal ward and was already planning on strategies that would give her as little contact with the woman as possible. She loathed her intensely, although from what she could gather, she wasn't the only one. The antagonism between them had been almost instantaneous, because she realised very quickly that Sister Frenchit's obsession with order, discipline and rigorous planning made it almost impossible to slide under her radar. Sister Frenchit's uncanny ability to hone in on anything that was out of alignment in the planning and running of her ward gave little scope for anyone who dared to challenge that equilibrium. It was inevitable that there would be clashes between them from day one.

Stella was one of a minority of Midwives who was not afraid of Sister Frenchit. In fact, because she knew it wound her up so much, she went out of her way to upset the icy, controlled exterior of her navy-clad nemesis. She enacted her vexation with care, waiting until Sister Frenchit was not on duty. Incidents were, at first, minor and not easy to pin down. A blood test report would go missing, requests for X-ray reports were sent to other departments, twenty-four-hour urine collections, stored in huge demijohns in the sluice, would disappear, or be so reduced in volume that concerns about a patient's kidney function were voiced on more than one occasion, resulting in yet more tests for the now very worried patient. Multiple tellings-off from Sister Frenchit to innocent staff and patients alike created an atmosphere of tension that was akin to treading on a long path of broken glass.

Stella loved it. She watched the growing frustration of Sister Frenchit and the misery of the staff who were on the receiving end of her undeserved verbal accusations with a satisfaction that was becoming almost the highlight of her day. Her photographic memory had held her in good stead and its one advantage with Sister Frenchit was that she could repeat parrot-like, in perfect order, whatever Sister Frenchit demanded of her.

One day, when lectures in the large classroom had finished and she was the last one to leave, she had noticed a pile of documents on the tutor's desk at the front of the classroom. On closer examination she realised they were a large stack of old examination papers with model answers often used as a practice run for students who were about to sit their finals. She scooped the lot up and put them into her bag and had then started to use them when tests came up as they did regularly.

Being able to access almost perfect answers to the

most commonly asked examination questions helped to disguise the fact that she didn't understand the ramifications of what any of it meant. She could talk the talk, but that was all. Clinical diagnosis or treatment planning was a big blank hole in her grey matter that would one day threaten the very lives of those she was meant to uphold.

Chapter Thirteen

Penny had completed her three months working on the postnatal floors and her next allocation was to work on the Labour Ward and Progress Department. The Progress Department was really just one big sorting house. Admissions came from a variety of sources, none of which was foreseeable. Patients with problems could be transferred in from home, from other wards in the hospital, from surrounding smaller maternity units, or from the Labour Ward itself if its beds were full and a Caesarean section patient needed some closer observation for a few hours. Inductions of labour would be transferred downstairs to Progress when established labour was diagnosed, so often there would be a number of bed-bound patients, tethered by their intravenous drips.

She walked up the corridor to the sister's office in the Progress Department and deposited her cloak and bag in the wall cupboard. The ward clerk was busy on the phone, and she wondered where the rest of the staff were. She mouthed a question at Chris, who was still on the phone, who silently gesticulated towards the bathroom areas, reserved for use by pregnant women.

Mystified, Penny walked back out of the door and around the corner to the nearest bathroom.

She pushed open the doors and was met with a noisy group of laughing Midwives and auxiliaries, all gathered around the bath. Lying in a very soapy, bright pink mixture of bubbles and foam, in full uniform, and with a necklace made up of individual enemas tied around her neck, was the lovely Staff Midwife Hoolihan who Penny had worked with earlier. A wheelchair decorated with tied-on cardboard bedpan inners and balloons, and a hand-painted sign that said 'almost married', was waiting for its recipient. It was customary for significant life events amongst staff to be celebrated in this way and even the medical fraternity joined in.

Towels were dropped onto the floor so that the dripping Midwife could squelch her way out of the bath and onto the wheel-chair where her colleagues tied her hands onto the armrests with crepe bandages. She was last seen being pushed up the corridor towards the canopy at the hospital's main entrance, where she was positioned for half an hour much to the amusement of staff and visitors. Eventually, she was released into the warmth of an old dressing-gown, and following a shower and change of uniform, was soon back to start her shift.

A notable event had occurred the previous year when one of the junior doctors was also getting married. His colleagues took him on a pub-crawl the night before his wedding day. Well after midnight, they returned with him to the Labour Ward which fortunately was very quiet. They commandeered a labour room and placed him in the lithotomy position, which, for the uninitiated, involves placing the patient flat on their back and placing each foot, knees bent, into a leather supportive strap, mimicking the position required to perform a forceps delivery.

With his genitals exposed, the young doctor was treated to a full pubic shave, his genital area then painted with gentian violet, a bright purple, deeply staining liquid, used for a variety of skin conditions. He was very inebriated and sleepy, and he was left on the Labour Ward to be found later by the night Superintendent of Midwifery when doing her rounds. She reported the incident and the next day a group of very hung-over doctors and medical students were seen leaving a meeting with the head of Midwifery and two of the Consultant Obstetricians before leaving to go and get changed into their wedding finery.

Five hours later, with no chance of a coffee break, and a morning full of admissions from home, Penny was able to go for lunch and meet up with Sylvia and Rosie. It was rare that they all managed to be together and lovely to catch up on each other's gossip. They sat in the coffee room, clutching welcome mugs of tea, munching on sandwiches and chatting noisily about family and friends.

One of the subjects was, of course, the poor Midwife who had been suspended from duty pending investigation. They all knew who she was and none of them believed for one minute that she was guilty of malpractice. A close friend of hers had told them, briefly, what she had been accused of and they were as shocked as everyone who got to know any details. Complete and utter privacy of the ups and downs of one's personal life was rare in the maternity unit, as its internal grapevine was more efficient than even the most updated, automated system.

If a Midwife was accused of malpractice, although gossip might be rife, the detailed examination that inevitably followed was shrouded in an atmosphere of tight-lipped solemnity. Accused staff were told not to communicate with anyone else and were, effectively, isolated at home and deprived of the very support they desperately needed – their own colleagues. Decisions and actions taken were scrutinised with a fine tooth-comb, supported by statements. Conclusions of all the circumstances that contributed to a maternal or foetal disaster were rarely shared as a learning experience for the rest of the staff.

Groups of Midwives and students, meeting up for breaks or when writing up their records, inevitably also turned their gossip towards the case of the accused Midwife, and it was no different for the three friends. They mulled over what they had heard and wondered how they would feel if accused of anything, or complained about. Rosie knew that she had been working on the Labour Ward around the time the accused was supposed to have delivered sub-standard care and there was something that kept niggling at her memory bank, something she couldn't quite put her finger on. She tried hard to remember what it was, willing herself to grab hold of the detail that eluded her, but it wouldn't come.

Just park it, she told herself, the memory will come back when I'm not thinking about it. The three friends finished their shared break and returned to their allocated areas of practice.

When Penny returned to the Progress Department, the late shift staff were on duty, boosting the workforce for a few hours as the early and late shifts overlapped. It was fortuitous that extra staff were briefly available and not one, but two Consultant Obstetricians happened to be on the Labour Ward suite of rooms. A patient who had just delivered her ninth baby was bleeding heavily. The delivery of the third stage of labour, that of delivering the placenta or afterbirth, had been difficult. Separation from the side wall of the uterus had been delayed and the organ that had nourished a baby had not fully relinquished its attachment to the life-supporting organ still inside the mother's uterus.

Although most of the afterbirth was finally delivered with great difficulty, the overworked, overstretched womb was not contracting effectively. The cross-muscle fibres that should effectively seal off any bleeding points in the uterine muscle could not come into play if the uterine muscles failed to contract. It was crucial that the muscles surrounding the womb contracted or bleeding would continue. Medical staff were concerned that some of the placenta might still be attached inside the womb, and if it was, that was the cause of the failure of the uterine muscle to do its job.

To make matters worse, the woman's haemoglobin levels were low and she was anaemic. The oxygen-carrying capabilities of her red blood cells were diminished as well as a resulting low blood volume caused by excessive bleeding that could threaten the life of the patient. Theatre was being prepared and Penny was instructed to be an extra pair of hands alongside the very experienced and permanent theatre staff who were already girding their loins for what looked like a couple of difficult hours.

Penny was very relieved that she was a just cog in a very large wheel of staff who would be supporting the medical team inside the theatre. She knew this could be a life or death situation for the mother if her haemorrhaging couldn't be brought under control. She hurried to the changing rooms, knowing that time was of the essence for the patient. She had heard one of the most experienced Midwives on the Labour Ward reporting the details of the case to the doctors and the theatre staff and it scared her just listening to it. The woman's blood pressure was beginning to drop and she was still bleeding vaginally, copious amounts of blood, with huge clots. She had a drip in each arm, with blood volume expander being pumped in.

Earlier, blood had begun to seep over the edge of the bed, soaking the sheets she was lying on when

Mercy, one of the cleaners, had pushed open the door to see if there were any dirty tea cups that needed collecting. She had literally been stopped in her tracks at the door by the volume of blood on the floor.

The Anaesthetist was already in theatre, preparing the drugs he would need to put his patient to sleep so that the Consultant could start on the very delicate job of scraping unwanted tissue off the inside walls of the patient's uterus.

Penny had changed into green theatre trousers and tunic top and found a pair of theatre clogs that actually fitted her, and joined Beryl at the row of scrubbing up sinks, glad to see a face she knew. The place was a hive of activity as six other members of the team quickly and silently scrubbed up and in record time donned their gowns, masks and gloves. The patient was wheeled in by the porters and placed onto the theatre bed. Penny could see how pale she looked; she was almost white. There were anxious looks shared silently between the numerous grades of staff, with just eye contact between them.

Penny's job was to double-check that all the packs of swabs that were used were counted when they were opened and counted after they were used. Each swab, soaked in blood after swabbing inside the body, or mopping up blood that was trickling out of the body, would then need to be hung individually upon a stainless-steel rack near to the theatre bed. It was absolutely vital that the numbers of gauze swab packs opened tallied with the numbers used and counted. It was easy to miss a swab or leave one inside the cavity of the body. When soaked with blood, they were difficult to see, but if left in, could cause massive infection.

The Anaesthetist had now sedated his patient and was busy putting an intubation tube down her throat, attaching it to an oxygen supply and starting to monitor his patient's vital signs. The amount of blood still leaking out of her body had not abated. Penny was at the bottom end of the bed where used swabs were thrown into a bowl by her feet. She was getting soaked in the woman's blood as she continually lifted swabs and placed them on the stand. The front of her gown was wet with it, as were her arms.

Two units of blood, one for each arm, were being run through the drip at a really fast rate as the bleeping monitor showed that the woman's blood pressure was starting to drop and her pulse to rise as her body tried unsuccessfully to stabilise the results of not having enough blood in her circulation.

As soon as the woman was anaesthetised the Consultant Obstetrician had swiftly placed his left hand on the woman's abdomen and inserted his right hand inside the woman's genital tract. He pushed his fingers further inside, removing more blood clots as they gathered at the back of the vagina. With the gentlest of touches, his sensitive fingers encountered the neck of the womb. He felt around the cavity he had just entered, searching for missing bits of placental tissue that, if removed, would save the woman's life.

He inwardly allowed himself to breathe a small sigh of relief as his fingers found the life-threatening tissue, and he began to carefully extract it from the inside of the patient's birth canal. The only sound heard inside the theatre was the ticking of the clock on the wall that was witness to events that the public would never know about. Finally all the placental tissue was out. Staff could be heard breathing a sigh of relief. More ergometrine was given intramuscularly to help the lax uterus to contract and inwardly seal off the bleeding points. Unfortunately, it didn't.

She still carried on bleeding. As her vital signs deteriorated, the Anaesthetist began to physically squeeze the blood into the intravenous giving set, sited in each of the mother's arms, aided by a junior doctor. More blood was requested. The Consultant gently palpated the mother's uterus which was still not firmly contracted. His options were diminishing by the minute. Penny saw him then carry out a manoeuvre that was performed when all else had failed.

He placed a hand over the top of the woman's symphysis pubis joint and, using his other hand, palpated the soft uterus abdominally, pushing his fingers behind it and then pressing the organ forward towards where his other hand was, effectively compressing the uterus between his hands. Fortunately, his patient was fully sedated and so did not suffer the extreme discomfort that this manoeuvre would have caused. He was externally clamping down hard on a uterus that had not effectively contracted, squeezing it between his hands to stem the flow of blood, giving the woman's clotting mechanism a chance to recover from the continual assault on its function. All of the staff who watched him knew it was a last-ditch manoeuvre.

There was utter silence in the theatre except for the bleeping of life-saving monitors. Penny's theatre gown was so wet with blood it was beginning to stick to her as it started to dry out from the heat of the theatre lights. Adrenalin was coursing through her veins. She had been assiduous in her counting of opened and used swabs, hanging them in groups of five as they were used. The effort of concentrating was beginning to tell on her.

Slowly, so very slowly, the flow of blood diminished, the patient's blood pressure began to inch upwards and the tension eased a little in the theatre.

As the patient's condition stabilised, the Consultant showed signs of preparing to finishing his administrations, and Penny checked her swabs. It was immediately obviously that one was missing. She took a deep breath in, and in a loud firm voice that she somehow managed to stop from shaking said 'Can I have your attention please!'

There was silence and all faces turned towards her.

'There's one swab missing.'

The exhausted Consultant turned a bleary eye on her.

'I don't think so, Staff. I got them all out.'

Penny persisted. She was still quaking inside, disagreeing with a Consultant as a very junior member of staff took a lot of courage, but she stuck to her guns.

'I'm very sure there is, there's definitely one missing.'

The Consultant was tired and not meaning to sound condescending. He performed another internal examination and pushing his fingers to the back of the woman's vagina he immediately found it, tucked into the posterior fornices of the vagina. He pulled it out and held it up for all to see.

'You were right, and I'm glad you noticed,' was all he said to Penny, simply because of his emotional exhaustion and continual scrutiny of his patient.

He wearily stepped back, stripped off his gloves and gave instructions for a barrage of blood tests to be carried out immediately on his patient. The clots of blood that littered the area on and around the bed had to be collected so that an estimation of the patient's blood loss could be documented. The mother would not be leaving the theatre any time soon as her observations, although improved, were not stable enough for her to be transferred around to a Labour Ward bed, let alone on a ward. A patient's collapse, after such an extensive assault on their body, was not unknown, and would catch inexperienced staff by surprise.

Penny was no longer needed as the full time theatre staff took over the rest of the woman's care. She stripped off her soiled gown, mask and gloves and deposited them into the theatre's soiled linen trolley. She used the shower facility in the theatre changing room to remove the blood that had soaked through her scrubs, relishing the brief respite of cleansing warm water, before putting on her uniform and returning to the Progress Department. During her couple of hours' absence, the Labour Ward had turned into a scene mimicking Dante's hell.

Every bed was full. One admission had been involved in a road traffic accident and was threatening to go into premature labour; another had foolishly climbed a pair of step ladders to get something out of her loft and, losing her balance, had fallen heavily from eight steps up. The ambulance staff had brought in a lady, who, phoning from a call box, said her husband had savagely beaten her in a drunken rage and she was scared the baby might be hurt, as he had also repeatedly kicked her in the stomach. Two induction ladies were breathing heavily into their entonox masks, obviously progressing well in labour, and Sister Frenchit was telephoning, trying to book the one vacant bed, insisting that her room's patient be given priority.

Penny donned a plastic apron over her uniform, and automatically began to issue instructions to student Midwives and auxiliaries who were supporting her. She suddenly realised how competently and smoothly she was functioning. It was a deeply satisfying realisation that her long-standing lack of confidence was rapidly disappearing and no longer worried her. She was actually enjoying herself. Although her incident in the theatre was a minor one, it was a turning-point for her confidence development. With that affirmation lifting her spirits no end, she hurried over to bed two where her patient was shouting 'I want to push…' and joined the rest of her colleagues on a shift whose demands none of them would forget in a hurry.

The next morning Penny arrived for the start of her early shift, still shattered from the previous day's workload. She hadn't slept well, but was getting used to those work moments that had no rhyme or reason to their predictability or intensity. She hung her cloak up in the big wall cupboard and was hopeful that the ensuing quietness was a sign that they weren't busy. She looked at the admissions book on the desk and saw that there were only two ladies occupying beds, one diagnosed as a urinary tract infection whose symptoms were mimicking premature labour, and the other who had possible ruptured membranes at thirty weeks, but so far, no one had seen any evidence of leaks of fluid.

It was also extraordinarily quiet outside the office. Usually there was a continuous clatter of trollies, porters and cleaners hurrying to and fro, and staff chatting as they came on or went off duty. Recently delivered women, clutching their precious infants, would be pushed in wheelchairs past the Progress office door on their way to the lifts which would take them up to the postnatal floors. The quiet atmosphere was one of a middle of the night lull, not one of a busy day about to burst into action.

Penny stuck her head out of the door and saw a mixed group of staff standing outside the theatre doors. Even from a distance she could tell there was something wrong. She could see that Sister Francis, who had also mentored her as a student Midwife, was standing next to Mr Baxter, the most senior of all the Consultant Obstetricians. There was Beryl from theatre and two other Midwives whose names she couldn't remember, all huddled together in a group. She started to walk down the corridor towards them and as she approached they all turned to face her, silent. As she reached the group, the inner doors of the theatre were opened by two of the porters. The view that was momentarily framed within the open doors would stay with Penny forever.

The stainless-steel theatre bed that she had stood by for hours the day before was shrouded completely in a white sheet, starkly outlining the unmistakeable outline and contours of a female body. At the same time she realised that everyone, except Mr Baxter, was crying openly, eyes red and puffy from prolonged periods of grief. The outpouring of tears was so copious, it was hard to watch.

Penny clutched Beryl's arm, distressed and alarmed, and gave her a hug as Beryl, stumbling through her tears, outlined what had happened. The lady from yesterday, who had bled so heavily, had started to bleed again, massively, even though the uterus had finally contracted the day before. She had bled so much over the last twenty-four hours, she had used up all of the clotting factors in her blood as her body tried to cope with the continuous bleeding.

A turning-point had been reached whereby no matter how much blood was pumped back into a body, it would just not be able to reverse the crippling effect of the malfunctioning clotting process. Vital signs had deteriorated rapidly, and the mother had suffered a massive cardiac arrest from which there had been no recovery.

Penny was devastated, tears forming in her eyes. She couldn't believe it. She choked back a sob as the doors from the main corridor opened and a Supervisor of Midwives appeared, her arm around and supporting a weeping man who could hardly stand up. From her memory of him the day before, he had aged twenty years. Mr Baxter approached him, along with Sister Francis, and they quietly escorted him towards the theatre doors so that he could say a last farewell to his wife, who had cheerily hugged him the day before and said, 'Don't worry, duck. I'll be back home tomorrow.' He didn't know how he was going to be strong enough to face up to the awful task of telling his eight children that their mother would never be coming home again and that his newborn would never feel its mother's caresses or kisses.

A maternal death, although very common in Third World countries, was more of a rarity in the Western World. An atmosphere of gloom and despondency settled on not just the Labour Ward area, but on the whole of the hospital. Birth was usually about life, joy, new beginnings, planning for the future. The way that a maternal death affected almost everyone in the building was akin to the way a family was left reeling after the ripples of a tragedy continued to batter the senses of relatives near and far. It would be years later before Penny realised that the many teams in the six-storey building worked, played and pulled together just like any family unit. Tragedies and disasters affected them all and they drew closer, just as triumphs and achievements were celebrated by all. They were, she realised, like so many before her, her second family.

Three weeks later, the congregation in the church,

who were paying their respects to a woman who was taken from this earth far too soon, stood as the coffin entered the door. The funeral service was packed with members of hospital staff, including Penny, who sobbed so much it made her feel ill, especially when she saw eight children being led in, each escorted or held by a relative. Although the dedicated hospital staff had been unable to save their mother, she thought the least she could do was to pay homage to the life she had lived. She would strive, as a Midwife, to give the best care she was capable of, so that no other family would be deprived of their mother, wife or sister so cruelly as this one.

Chapter Fourteen

Charles Merton was on a high, albeit a drug-induced one. His need for opiates was growing faster than his ability to acquire them and he was becoming desperate. After his meeting with the head of Midwifery services, he realised that a drastic re-evaluation of his procurement of drugs was needed, and in the end, it had been relatively easy.

He invented a long-standing back problem that gave him severe sciatic pain. His Consultant colleagues were able to provide him with private, repeat prescriptions for strong painkillers in tablet issue, an acceptable form of practice amongst the medical fraternity at the time. He chose colleagues who worked in different disciplines to himself and who were based across the hospital site, resulting in a number of prescriptions that ensured a constant supply.

He then used community-based pharmacies around the city to pick up supplies and, with relief, slipped into the comforting routine of not having to worry where his next fix was coming from. He fully embraced the mind-numbing, peaceful, sleepy state that followed the ingestion of his little pill saviours, whose effects lasted for five or six hours at a time.

He was unaware of the increasingly frequent effects that his drug dependency was having on his behaviour. He had been arriving late for his theatre lists, caused by sudden bouts of exhaustion that demanded an eyes closed, ten-minute revival in his office. Except that, frequently, it wasn't just ten minutes. He would nod off, and then wake with a start, confused, still drowsy, half an hour later. Consultants of his seniority and standing were often delayed, but good communication alerted the Labour Ward staff if delays occurred because of emergencies elsewhere.

He would give no warning and so, regularly, he wasn't the most popular name to be seen on roster lists. His change of behaviour created a few grumblings of discontent amongst the Labour Ward staff, but he was not challenged in any way – his seniority and the pedestal upon which all members of the medical fraternity were placed, protected him. He was beginning to find concentrating for any length of time difficult, which he put down to an ever-increasing workload and a high status, high maintenance wife who, with her constant nagging, was pushing him into spending even longer hours in his hospital office. On two occasions, he had fallen asleep in there only to be awakened by his secretary coming on duty at eight o' clock in the morning who was faced with the rare sight of a dishevelled, unshaved man in a very crumpled suit who bore little resemblance to the articulate, well-groomed professional who strutted through his domain like a cockerel herding his hens.

Rosie was walking down the corridor. She had just purchased a chocolate snack from the WVS counter in the antenatal clinic and was in a hurry to get to the coffee room. She was passing the office of the Head Of Midwifery Services when her door opened, and she almost collided with the group of people who were just leaving. The Head of Midwifery was escorting an Indian couple, apparently man and wife, and the antenatal clinic interpreter, who was still chatting to the couple.

She apologised profusely, glancing at the couple as she did so and a flash of recognition unearthed a memory from the previous year. It was the lady who had ended up having a Caesarean for failure to progress and maternal distress. And suddenly she remembered the incident with her notes, the discrepancy of when a shot of Pethidine was given to the lady standing in front of her. The timing placed the accused Midwife, whose signature was next to the written record, on the Labour Ward with the woman, but Rosie knew now that couldn't be so as she had watched the accused Midwife go off duty at least twenty minutes earlier.

Knowing that her memory could have implications for the suspended Midwife she sought out Sister Francis, who was busy writing up yet more notes in the sitting-room. Fortunately, there was no one else present, and she recounted the incident to her.

'I think we need to go and have a conversation with Mrs Montgomery, and sooner rather than later,' she said, and seconds later they were outside the door of the Head Of Midwifery Services.

They entered at her command and were seated immediately in armchairs next to her desk.

'What can I do for you, Sister Francis, and who's this you have with you?'

A pair of intelligent grey eyes appraised her, speculatively.

Rosie was introduced, who by now was feeling very apprehensive. She felt as though it was she who had just committed some grave clinical disaster and was on trial.

'Tell Mrs Montgomery what you have just told me,' instructed Sister Francis.

Taking a deep breath to calm herself, Rosie recounted what she had told Sister Francis while Mrs Montgomery sat back in her chair and listened intently and then clarified some points with a series of questions. It was the first time Rosie had had any contact with the Head of Midwifery, and she had certainly never stepped over the threshold of her office door before. She felt very intimidated and, if truth be known, more than a bit scared. She needn't have worried. The questioning was non-judgmental, purely fact-finding, with probing, questions that drew out of Rosie information she didn't know she'd even remembered until asked.

When she had finished questioning Rosie, Mrs Montgomery sat in silence for a little while, coming to terms with the fact that someone was falsifying records and misappropriating drugs, both very serious crimes. She thanked the young Midwife for coming forward and said that she would need to provide a formal, written statement, outlining in detail the information that she had just shared.

'A Supervisor of Midwives and your union rep from the Royal College of Midwives will help you with the finer points of preparing a statement, so don't worry about it,' she said kindly, showing her visitors to the door. After the Midwives had left her office, she made a number of phone calls and then went to visit the Labour Ward manager. They both had a lot to talk about.

Sylvia unlocked the padlock that chained the drugs' trolley to the wall by the Midwife station. She opened up the trolley using the key that was one of many attached to the large bunch that was pinned securely to the inside of her dress pocket. Rows of bottles of medication that were currently being prescribed for inpatients were stored on the trolley, along with a file that held a prescription sheet for every patient who was being treated on the Ward.

Becoming familiar with the huge variety of drugs and their different doses, as well as understanding the unfamiliar jargon of how a prescription was written, was quite a challenge, and as a student she remembered thinking that she would never in a million years become competent at this particular task. Through training and continuous, thrice-daily drugs' rounds, she had slowly assimilated in her brain all she needed to know, and now she was confident in carrying out an important part of the Ward's daily routine.

It was a shame she couldn't say the same about student Midwife Stella Steel. Her reservations about her practice had not diminished since she had become aware of them on the Labour Ward a few months ago. The usual, three-monthly rotation to different Ward areas had resulted in both of them being allocated to Sister Frenchit's Antenatal Ward and Sylvia anticipated that sparks would fly.

She was not wrong, and was alarmed to see that Stella didn't seem affected by the almost continuous reprimands she received from Sister Frenchit. Any other student would have been in floods of tears and shaking in her boots, but not Stella. She seemed to relish it, and almost invite criticism, which made Sister Frenchit even more tetchy and short-tempered.

Sylvia pushed the trolley down the corridor into Room One, opened up the file of patients' prescriptions, and prepared to dish out a variety of tablets and liquid medication to the six women who were housed there. As she worked her way around the room, greeting each patient by name, Mrs Reardon, occupying the bed by the window, was on her hands and knees, the contents of her locker on the floor and on her bed. When Sylvia asked her if she had a problem, she said that she had lost her gold earrings. She had them in the day before, she said, and took them off in the bathroom when she had a shower. She thought she had picked them up, but they were nowhere to be found. She was really upset, and Sylvia promised she would ask the rest of the staff to keep a lookout for them whilst moving around the Ward. She finished her drugs round without further incident and mentioned the loss of the earrings during the staff report.

Whilst Sylvia was pushing her trolley around the antenatal floor Elizabeth Montgomery, Mr Baxter, a senior consultant, the Manager of the Labour Ward and one of the Supervisors of Midwives met in the large classroom armed with a pile of statements, the results of intensive investigations, three sets of patients' notes and copies of staff rosters of all grades. They studied, cross-referenced, and plotted the events during the time frame of care given to the ladies who had complained about their inadequate pain relief. Rosie's statement had been crucial in underlining that there was a big problem. It had been verified that the Midwife in question definitely could not have given at least one of the doses of Pethidine. She also queried and questioned the validity of what was purported to be her signature, saying again that she bought her red pens in batches and that they were a specific shade of red which did not match up with the writing in the notes. All of the patients said they had definitely not been given extra pain relief when they had asked for it. Someone was faking signatures and not giving a morphine-derived drug. A member of staff was taking Pethidine for personal use.

Three hours later they had made little headway. Elizabeth Montgomery felt the beginning of a migraine and the Labour Ward manager was at her wits' end at the thought of the integrity of the Dangerous Drugs Act being severely compromised in her department. As they sat there, the desks in front of them full of documents and reports, Mr Baxter picked up a batch of staff rosters for the days when the three ladies were labouring. He was tired, still had a ward round to attend to, and had a high-risk patient in labour who, he knew, would be presenting with big problems sooner rather than later.

He scanned the off-duty sheets for his medical staff for the umpteenth time, a gesture of seeming to do something, anything, and was about to return them to the pile when a small detail caught his eye. The one member of staff who had been on duty at the time all the three women were labouring was Charles Merton.

Impossible, not the golden boy of research, the academic who also had innumerable papers published, the ladies' man who had half the female staff in the palm of his hand. God, he must be tired. He pushed the thought aside, irritable with himself for clutching at straws, and excused himself, saying he would talk to them again the following day.

On the Labour Ward, Mr Baxter's high-risk patient was being examined by Charles Merton who was on call. The lady in question was carrying a small-for-dates baby inside her uterus. She was thirty-seven weeks pregnant and it was estimated from clinical examination that her baby weighed only four pounds. The baby was not growing as it should; a dangerous situation, as babies who were compromised in this way could, with little warning, suddenly become deeply distressed, especially during labour. A decision was made to induce labour, the extra-uterine environment considered to be safer than staying inside the mother's body. A Syntocinon drip was inserted into her arm, dripping its powerful concoction into the woman's bloodstream, stimulating the uterus to start its rhythmical tightening.

She had been on the Labour Ward for a number of hours now and little progress had been made. Charles knew that a long drawn-out labour was on the cards, a situation he really didn't want at the best of times, but especially now. He was exhausted and not sleeping well and he was in desperate need of his daily fix. He scanned the patient's notes and decided he could up the dosage of the Syntocinon. If he ran the drip through a bit faster for a short length of time, he could really get the labour established quicker and he wouldn't need to be around for half the night.

The pull of his office, his daily fix, and his exhaustion clouded his judgement and his clumsy manipulation of the intravenous infusion-giving set resulted in the overgenerous opening of the valve that controlled the amount of the drug entering the woman's body. He didn't notice that she had a high dose of Syntocinon added to the infusion she was receiving, neither did he document any change to the drug regime in the patient's notes or notice that she had had a previous Caesarean section, her last pregnancy in fact. He would just have a quick ten-minute break and then come back. He would manually reset the drip rate and no one would be any the wiser. Without a backward glance, he left the labour room as the intravenous infusion started to empty its dangerous dose of Syntocinon into the woman's bloodstream.

Just around the corner in the Progress Department, Penny was rushed off her feet dealing with the mass of inductions that had been carried out. Progress beds were rapidly filling up. It was going to be another 'delivery on a trolley day', she surmised, they were so stuffed to the gills with patients. She had taken a tray loaded with dirty dishes into Mercy's kitchen area only to be accosted by Mercy for making a mess and creating yet more work for her. Mercy's kitchen was her castle and on really busy days it was difficult to keep up with the never-ending tea and toast trays. Space was limited at the best of times and work surfaces covered with piles of unwashed crockery created the same effect on Mercy as a personal insult.

Feeling guilty, Penny started to try and stack the dishes, and another tongue-lashing ensued with Mercy accusing her of 'taking over my job now!' She apologised profusely, bumping into a group of new medical students loitering in the corridor on her way out of the kitchen.

The medical students stood out in their pristine white coats and newly purchased stethoscopes, which hung around their necks like a badge of honour. Even though they conducted themselves with an almost puppy-like demeanour of wanting to please, very soon they too discovered the length and breadth of Mercy's tongue.

Walking up the corridor, Penny was pleased and surprised to see Sylvia passing the door on her way to the Labour Ward and she explained that she had been borrowed for a few hours from her usual ward to support the workload which was beginning to reach unmanageable proportions. With a bit of luck, they might manage a coffee break together in the Midwives' sitting-room. With that simple pleasure planned and anticipated, both of them returned to their respective areas of work.

Mr Baxter's high-risk patient was beginning to struggle. She felt decidedly unwell and braced herself for the onslaught of pain that was now accompanying every contraction. That new doctor had certainly stirred things up. She had progressed from barely discernible tightenings to very frequent, incredibly painful contractions every two three minutes, with hardly any respite in between.

She was as keen as the Midwives and doctors to get into established labour and get her baby out as she knew about the baby's risks. But she couldn't remember any of her past labours being this painful. There was no gradual build-up where she had time to adjust to the pain, to alter her breathing to help her cope. The pain was deep-seated, and it felt as if someone was pushing a knife deep into her gut. It made her catch her breath with such intensity she had difficulty in breathing.

When the doctor had readjusted her drip, he had pushed her bedside locker aside as he located and adjusted the rate of her infusion. Her nurse-call button was now out of her reach. She clenched her teeth and her fists as another wave of agonising pain hit her. She started to sweat, and a fine tremor was starting to accompany the contractions. A feeling of panic was slowly starting to engulf her, and she let out a strangled cry as a particularly vicious spasm felt as though she was being torn in two.

Charles Merton was sitting upright in his high back, swivel chair. He was fast asleep, and his head had lolled to one side. An opened bottle of pills lay on his desk in front of him; his little life-savers had worked their magic. His breathing was deep and regular and he looked for all the world like a man at home on a Sunday afternoon, enjoying a siesta after his lunch. He frowned in his sleep and stirred, eyelids flickering, as he dreamed his drug-induced dreams.

Sylvia was caring for two low-risk labouring women, both situated in rooms next to each other, and they were both progressing quite quickly. It was going to be a race between who delivered first. They were both using their entonox masks really efficiently, sucking in great lungfuls of nitrous oxide and oxygen. The euphoric effect allowed them to remain in control as their contractions built to a peak. They were both confident, experienced mothers with histories of normal deliveries previously. Their close proximity meant that she could still monitor both of her patients, especially as she had the help of Heather, a lovely nursery nurse who mothered the women and babies in her care as much as her own mother still mothered her. When the time came, Heather would be her assistant, opening packs for the delivery, checking the infant resuscitation trolley and taking the baby from her after delivery. They had worked together before and their respective knowledge of each other's responsibilities and boundaries resulted in seamless, relaxed teamwork.

The late shift were gathering by the Midwife station, preparing to receive the report of the morning's activities. Groups of medics and Midwives clustered around, waiting for an update on all of the occupants of the eight labour rooms. Sylvia stayed with her patients as one of them was fast approaching full dilatation and would be wanting to push soon. As she stood by her patient's side, wiping her face with a cool face cloth, rubbing her lower back and reassuring her she would soon be ready to push, she reflected on the deep sense of satisfaction that delivering babies gave her. The almost continual layer of anxiety and nervousness that never lay far away during those early months of qualified practice were now kept in their proper place, emerging only when they should, after detecting or anticipating a problem. She was learning rapidly to listen to that sixth sense, when something niggled at her that she couldn't quite put her finger on. She respected those niggles and, years later, she would thank whichever gods were looking over her shoulder, and the insistence of those niggles that had saved the lives of more than one mother and baby.

Penny dashed around the corner to the Labour Ward through the scrum of staff waiting to hear the report, looking for Sylvia. Beryl, from theatre, informed her she was in Room One with her patient. She walked there, tapped on the door and pushed her head through just in time to see Sylvia clamping and cutting the cord of the baby she had delivered. It was a girl, already crying and announcing her arrival, music to a mother's and a Midwife's ears.

'It looks like we won't be lunching together,' she said, 'but I hope to see you for a coffee break.' And to the mother, she added, 'And you have a gorgeous baby!'

She closed the door and walked to the bottom of the corridor in order to exit the Ward via a side-door which medical staff often used as a short cut from their residences. The door to Room Four, at the end, was closed and there were no sounds coming from within, unusual when a room was occupied by a patient. She casually looked in the small window, inset into the door, and could see the patient had slipped down the bed and looked most uncomfortable. And she noticed that her bedside locker wasn't within her reach. She couldn't leave her like that, so she pushed the door open.

She approached the bed and realised immediately that something was very wrong. The patient was unconscious. She slammed her hand onto the emergency buzzer on the wall by the bed and the light over the door outside started to flash as the urgent sound rent the air, strident in its intensity. Penny noticed, as she pulled the pillows out from beneath the woman readying her for resuscitation, that her drip had run through completely and blood was beginning to backtrack up the tubing. Seconds later, the door was swung open and a Midwife and a senior Registrar ran in.

One look at the patient told them all they needed to know and what they needed to do.

An oxygen mask was quickly placed over the woman's face whilst the Registrar, with great difficulty, tried to insert a venous cannula into the woman's arm. Someone else was taking her blood pressure which was almost unrecordable; her pulse was also rapid and irregular. More staff arrived, including an Anaesthetist and a porter with a trolley, and in less than a minute the room was full.

Penny knew how seriously ill the patient was, watching her being intubated on the bed, the Anaesthetist trying to get an airway down the patient's throat as fast as possible. The use of the porter's trolley was abandoned in favour of pushing the patient on the bed straight into theatre and in less than five minutes she was on her way, staff pushing the bed on all sides, almost at a run, to get her there.

Mr Baxter had finished seeing his patients on the Antenatal Ward and made his way downstairs. He had been expecting a call, at the very least, from Charles Merton who he knew was there and would have been assessing his patient. It was a good hour at least since he had been in touch, and Mr Baxter was soon expected in the large classroom to give a lecture to the junior medical staff.

He wanted a full update on his patient before he became unavailable again in the confines of the classroom. He pushed through the double doors of the main corridor into pandemonium. The bed with his patient on it was frantically being manoeuvred through the theatre doors. He could see the theatre staff setting up for an emergency Caesarean section, their usual smooth, well-oiled routines seeming almost disjointed in their haste.

He caught the eye of the senior Registrar.

'I think it's a Couvelaire uterus, rock hard and impossible to palpate. No external signs of bleeding, but all vital signs severely compromised. No foetal heart heard.'

'I'm scrubbing up. Inform the classroom I'm no longer available, so they'll have to find someone else or cancel. And where the hell is Mr Merton?' And with that, Mr Baxter joined the team.

Penny was still in a state of shock after finding a collapsed patient whose survival chances, from the look of things, were looking grim. Her lunch break, along with everyone else's on the Ward, went out of the window. She was allocated immediately to fill the staffing gap and it was not until she snatched some tea and toast three hours later that she heard any updates. No one had emerged from theatre. As she stood in Mercy's kitchenette, the door opened and there was Sylvia, desperate herself for a quick brew, which from the look of things would be the only refreshment she would be getting during her shift.

'I've just seen Sid outside theatre. She has a ruptured uterus. A previous section scar burst. It looks from the records that the Midwife started her drip with a high dosage of Syntocinon and it ran through in record time; in fact, the unit controlling the rate of flow was completely open when you found her. There's going to be hell to pay for somebody. She's had massive overstimulation of her uterus from the Syntocinon which should have been on a really low dosage and low drip rate.'

Penny knew there was no point asking if the baby had survived; its blood supply would have been compromised almost immediately, with lethal consequences.

'Needless to say, they've had to do a hysterectomy, and they still don't know if she'll make it. Apparently, Mr Baxter's on the warpath. Charles Merton was supposed to be on call and re-evaluating her condition and progress, and he's not answering his bleep.'

Charles Merton was at that moment slowly emerging from a very deep fog of drug-induced sleep and lethargy. His vision was blurred and his mouth felt like the inside of a sewer. He rubbed his eyes, running a hand over his face, trying to ignore the pounding in his head which was making his brain shake inside his skull. It wouldn't go away, and he realised the pounding was coming from someone knocking furiously on his door. Still confused and dazed, he staggered up and, almost tripping over, reached the door and unlocked it. Outside was his secretary who had been knocking hard, and concerned at getting no answer had contacted Mr Baxter and the 'heavy squad' porters who appeared on the ward areas if any male visitors became abusive or violent. Merton stood there, still too intoxicated to be able to formulate any form of communication.

Mr Baxter pushed past him into the office without a word, taking in the scattered pills on the desk and the bottles of other medication that were lined up. He turned to look at the man in front of him whose life achievements had just been wiped out instantly.

He turned to the secretary. 'Call the police, Barbara, will you?'

And to the porters, 'Stay with him till they arrive.'

Chapter Fifteen

Rosie had missed seeing her friends on her lunch break and, on her way out of the building, called into the Labour Ward to see if they were still there. They were, both furiously writing up notes and carrying out post-delivery observations on their recently delivered mothers. Details of the afternoon's emergency had slowly filtered through the hospital and the arrival of a police car had raised the level of tongue-wagging even further; but as yet, very few people knew of any connection. It would be at least another hour before her two friends would be able to go off duty as theatre was still operating and some of the late shift were still in there, reducing the workforce for the rest of the Ward. She made plans to catch up with them both the following day before heading for the basement to get changed.

She was late, due to her detour, and there were very few people about; she had missed the usual frenzied scrum of the early shift all hurrying together to get out of the building. She sat down on the bench near to her locker, took her shoes off, and sat quietly for a few minutes, enjoying the brief respite. She heard the changing room door open and close and footsteps walking along the row of lockers that was hidden from her view. They stopped and she heard the rattle of a padlock. The footsteps continued, more rattles of padlocks followed and Rosie suddenly realised with a jolt that someone was trying all the locks. There followed an exasperated sigh and a coarse expletive that Sister Frenchit would definitely not have approved of.

Rosie stood up quietly and walked to the end of the row of lockers. She peered around the corner as the door swung open and someone else entered the room. She was just in time to see the exit of Stella Steel, brusquely pushing past the latecomer.

The following day, Rosie met up with Sylvia for a lunch break. As they walked briskly across the hospital site to the staff canteen, she told her what she had seen in the changing room the night before. Sylvia remembered the recent incident on her Ward of the missing earrings and began to wonder if they not only had a student who was failing to achieve her clinical competencies but who was a thief as well. They had no concrete evidence, but both of them were worried and didn't quite know what to do.

'All we can be is vigilant and try to keep an eye out for any other suspicious behaviour,' said Rosie, and with that they separated to return to their respective wards.

On her return to the Labour Ward, Sylvia walked down the corridor and realised that a small group of staff had gathered outside room six where her patient lay. She could hear violent swearing and scuffles, followed by the loud clash of a steel trolley being pushed hard into a ceramic sink. The person who two burly porters were trying to manhandle out of the room was so drunk she could smell the alcohol emanating from every pore of him from eight feet away. Stocky, unkempt, and unshaven, he was swaying on his feet and shaking a fist at the petrified mother on the bed while the auxiliary nurse in the room was trying to stop him approaching his wife.

'She's fucking coming home with me,' he snarled, and made a wild grab at her. Fortunately, both of the young porters had part-time jobs as bouncers at a local nightclub and were more than capable of restraining him. The amount of alcohol he had consumed made him less effective in his attempt to bully and domineer his wife, whom he had spent years abusing both physically and emotionally. His reflexes were slower and the alcohol clouded his judgement. Pushing him out of the door, both porters frogmarched him up the corridor as he struggled and shouted a string of vitriolic curses, which faded as he was unceremoniously removed from the premises and threatened with the police if he returned.

Breathing a sigh of relief, Sylvia rushed to comfort her patient, reassuring her that he wouldn't be allowed back into the Ward. She then spent some time trying to convince her to see a social worker who would try to get her a place in a woman's refuge.

The sad fact was that the incidence of domestic violence increased hugely during pregnancy, and this was not the first case that Sylvia had been involved in. During her community placement, she had been on call one night with her mentor Midwife, and a woman had phoned from a callbox, deeply distressed. They had driven there and found the heavily pregnant woman in a collapsed state and bleeding quite heavily from the kicking and beating her husband had given her. She had left the house whilst he was asleep and walked the streets until she found a phone box. They had called out the 'flying squad' – a small team of Midwife and Senior Registrar – who could give on the spot emergency treatment, enough to stabilise the patient's condition and get her transferred into hospital.

The array and complexity of pregnancies, and the different social circumstances of each woman and family, never ceased to amaze Sylvia. Every case was different, each presenting its own challenges. No day of work was ever the same. Communication was key; effective communication and the ability to very quickly cut through barriers of social norms and to find out what was needed and to act, often immediately. When she had the time for a quiet moment of self-reflection on the job that Midwives did, what she did, and the trust endowed in the profession, she realised it was an incredibly unique position to be in.

She could be meeting a patient whom she had never met before, in very challenging social circumstances, and then at once, sometimes to save a life, perform a very intimate examination that required the immediate acceptance of a stranger. The utter taboo of a woman's very private sexual organs, the most sacred part of a woman's femininity, being made accessible to a complete stranger, albeit a Midwife, highlighted the massive amount of trust that patients bestowed upon them.

Midwifery training, she decided, had two very distinct phases. The first was the two years of seeking knowledge in the training school, the anatomy and physiology and the treatments. The second phase, which was much longer and more complex, was the school of learning about the lessons of life, about the lives of women and their families, both segments of learning intimately entwined with the other. She doubted there was any assessment that could adequately prepare any Midwife for what the second phase of life experiences would throw at her; but then, that was the beauty and pull of each day. Would she swap that uncertainty and challenge for another more structured profession?

Never, she thought, never in a million years, and readjusting her starched cap she went around the corner to plead for the sustenance of a cup of tea from Mercy's kitchenette.

The atmosphere in Sister Frenchit's office was decidedly chilly, fast approaching sub-zero. She sat behind her desk, ramrod straight and fixed her piercing blue eyes on the individual who stood in front of her. She studied her intently, like a scientist looking closely through a microscope at some rare specimen, which in her eyes, she was. She hadn't encountered a specimen with so many undesirable traits as this one in a very long time.

'Student Midwife Steel, you are here in front of me, yet again. I have received complaints about you from patients.'

There was no response from Stella, not a flicker of emotion. She stood, looking straight at Sister Frenchit, and returned the stare. The silence in the office lengthened.

'Well, what do you have to say for yourself? You have seen the list of complaints that patients have reported. Do you have any explanation for your actions, or lack of them?'

The list of previous complaints, and the more recent ones, lay on Sister Frenchit's desk and she picked it up and quickly scanned down it. The use of swear words in front of patients, asking a woman who had delivered a stillborn baby if she wanted to feed, leaving a bottle of milk formula on her bedside locker, inaccurate blood pressure recordings, and falsifying readings in some instances which only came to light when three patients with very raised blood pressures had asked why they hadn't had their blood pressure checked that day. She had left a bedbound patient, who she was responsible for monitoring, for so long, waiting for a bedpan, that after frequent, ignored requests, she had been unable to wait and had urinated in her bed. She was still struggling to achieve accurate abdominal palpations, but could recite word-perfect sections of anatomy and physiology from Margaret Myles' textbook on the subject.

Stella readjusted her weight onto her other leg and breathed a big sigh. It was becoming very tedious working on the old spinster's ward. She never missed a trick and it was becoming more and more obvious that Sister Frenchit was honing in on her activities, and she'd rather she didn't. The stolen exam papers with their textbook answers had stood her in good stead up until now, but she had noticed that the very experienced eye of Mrs O'Neil, Senior Midwife tutor, was often turned on her in the classroom, frequently seeking her out to answer questions. She had struggled if the questions had been about treatment, resulting from a series of clinical assessments. She could recite by rote pure fact, for example, describe the anatomy of the female breast. Taking the next step forward by linking physiological changes with cause and effect and then making choices of what to do next were beyond her.

Sister Frenchit sat back in her chair, having received no further response from Stella. Silence still pervaded her office and the usually unnoticed tick of the wall clock became a prominent sound, reminiscent of a time bomb, slowly ticking down to its inevitable end.

Sister Frenchit straightened the file on the desk in front of her.

'I am going to arrange a meeting with Mrs O'Neil and you. I will be attending, along with your mentor Midwife. We will explore together your failed competencies and put together a plan of extra tuition and practical application.'

Stella's heart sank. There was no way she wanted to put herself out and spend even more time in activities that were just a means to an end.

'If you want to practise Midwifery and enter a profession that is held in great esteem, I suggest, Nurse Steel, that you pay more attention to the wants and needs of your patients. And can I draw specific attention to your choice, and use, of the English language when communicating with patients? At least try and use the correct anatomical phrases. Saying to a woman "get your arse up here" or "are your tits painful?" is completely unacceptable and will not be tolerated on my Ward. Is that clear?'

There was still no response from Stella, who had pursed her lips tightly together to stop herself, with great difficulty, from retorting with more blasphemy.

'Please close the door on the way out,' and with that Sister Frenchit closed the file in front of her, signalling an end to the meeting.

As the door closed, Sister Frenchit sighed. She could foresee an even greater uphill struggle with that one. Even so, there was no way any student who had been on her Ward would be leaving it without a rigorous immersion in good, solid practice. The battle was on, and over her dead body would that student fail to achieve her objectives when within her realm.

Thirty minutes later, out of pure spite and a deep-seated desire to get her own back on the old bag in the office, Stella Steel tucked a wedding ring, left on the side of a woman's locker, into her uniform pocket. She left the Ward, whistling under her breath, heading for the basement changing rooms. She couldn't wait to leave, as soon as possible, the cloying atmosphere of people she was beginning to detest.

Chapter Sixteen

It was three o'clock in the morning and Sylvia sat at the desk on the corridor, filing some blood test results. She was concentrating as she sifted through a variety of reports, all needing to go into the recipient's set of notes, illuminated by a little pool of light thrown by the lamp on her desk. She was in the middle of her once-a-year stint of night duty, a requirement expected of all staff in order to cover and offer a twenty-four-hour maternity service. The corridor lights were turned down to their lowest setting, creating shadow pockets along its length, and the day room lights and television, normally continually in use throughout the day, were turned off.

When the Ward was shut down for the night, babies were removed from their mothers' bedsides and wheeled in their Perspex cots into the nursery, one sited at each end of the Ward. This was to help mothers get some good quality sleep to aid their recovery. Those mothers who were breast-feeding would be awoken, if they requested it, to feed their babies, whilst the night staff would be responsible for giving a bottle-feed to all other babies in residence. Each of the twenty-eight beds was full, so she knew that she and the nursery nurse working alongside her were going to be busy later on, serenaded, no doubt, by the lusty cries of a number of babies demanding sustenance.

She filed the last blood test in its rightful place, thankful that Sister Frenchit had, during her training, instilled in her rigorous record-keeping and ward management skills. As a student, she had been required, day in and day out, to adhere to her strict, structured processes, and now she was glad. It came as no hardship to do it her way, and it had become second nature to do so.

She stood up, stretched, and started her hourly, quiet vigil of the mothers in her care by walking down the corridor to Room One. The lights were turned off and every bed had its curtains pulled around to give the women some privacy. The only sounds that could be heard, other than some mothers snoring, were the soft pressure noises that her rubber-soled shoes made on the synthetic floor covering. She listened, standing quietly, and satisfied, she repeated her routine, walking slowly and quietly into rooms with multiple beds and peering through the small glass aperture set into the doors of the single side rooms until she reached the other end of the ward, where her last scrutiny would be Room Twelve.

She walked quietly into the six-bedded room, where all was silent. She accessed the nursery via a door at the end of the room and found Heather, her colleague for the night, busy bathing a new-born. Because of the very regular staff rotation to different wards and departments, Midwives got to know each other, and other members of the multi-disciplinary team they worked with, very well. It was a pleasure, eventually, to get to know most of the people in the building, which made the unit as a whole even more cohesive in their day-to-day collaboration.

'It's going to take forever to get all the vernix off her,' said Heather. 'Just look, I've never seen a baby with so much! She looks like someone's taken a pound of lard and rubbed her all over with it!'

Sylvia laughed and agreed. The velvety, peach-like skin was one of the wonders of a new-born and it was in this condition at birth because of the presence of a thick, white, creamy substance called vernix. It was an important component of uterine life and protected a baby's skin in their fluid-filled environment. Usually, it was at its most prolific in the creases of armpits and groins, but some babies were born with extra generous coverings. Sylvia often surmised that if someone could produce a moisturising cream made out of vernix, they could make a fortune, so well did it perform its job of protecting the skin.

While Heather was busy drying her charge in a fluffy white towel, Sylvia walked back up the corridor and went into the milk kitchen where babies' feeds were prepared. The bottles were warmed up by standing them in a jug of hot water and a trolley was used to transport them down to the nursery. She loaded up and, returning to the nursery, settled down for a pleasant hour of feeding the babies who wanted it. At the other end of the corridor Heather was engaged in the same activity, as well as helping out a breast-feeding mother of twins who needed support in fixing her babies onto her breast.

Sylvia lifted the last baby up who had wanted feeding and, tucking a muslin nappy onto her left shoulder, winded her little bundle who had just emptied a full bottle of formula milk. She was rewarded with a resounding burp and a little posset of milk onto her nappy protection. The baby's eyelids were already closed and regular, rhythmic breathing confirmed that this little one was going to be in the

Land of Nod for the next few hours. She stood up and, locating baby's cot, tucked the sleeping bundle securely in.

She looked out of the nursery window onto the staff car park and, four floors up, admired the panoramic view. The sun was just beginning to rise, and she had witnessed some spectacular sunrises in times past. A small movement below caught her eye on the car park, and looking more closely she saw a car that looked familiar leaving it. She thought no more about it as a room buzzer attracted her attention and she hurried out of the door to answer the call for assistance.

Three nights later, just after midnight, Sylvia was busy admitting a patient who was recovering from a Caesarean section. The woman had endured a long, painful labour and made little progress. Her failure to progress was eventually diagnosed; it was caused by cephalo pelvic disproportion. The diameter of her baby's head would not pass through her pelvis, so no matter how long she laboured, it would be impossible for baby to be delivered vaginally. Weeks later, at her follow-up appointment, an X-ray would show that she had a male-type pelvis, whose inner dimensions were smaller and its shape quite different from that of a female pelvis.

Sylvia tucked her into bed again after changing her soiled incontinence sheet, and ensured she could reach her bedside buzzer. She lowered her bed backrest, plumped up her pillows, and, dimming the lights, wished the woman goodnight. She returned to her desk, grateful for the opportunity to sit for a few minutes. The workload had been non-stop since she had come on duty at nine o'clock. She heard the lift doors open and close, followed by the squeak of the hinges as the doors to the Ward were pushed open. Then it was silent again.

She continued writing up her records on the woman's condition in the Cardex system, subconsciously registering that she wasn't expecting anyone on the Ward. She finished her record-keeping, closed the Cardex and returned it to the drawer in the desk. She stood and turned at the same time as a large, male figure materialised behind her. He was so close she could smell alcohol and the stench of his unwashed body.

Shocked, she stumbled back, and bumped into the large metal trolley full of patients' notes that stood by the desk, which effectively trapped her in a corner with nowhere to go. Her mouth was dry, her pulse was racing, and she couldn't reach the emergency buzzer. She felt sick with fear as the man leaned forward and grabbed her arm. He had long, unkempt hair, a full, matted beard, and a very weather-beaten face. His clothes were literally rags and to say he smelt of unwashed body odour was the understatement of the year. The smell was so unpleasant that Sylvia reflexively gagged. She couldn't help it.

'I need a drink. You can get me a drink, can't you nurse?' He stumbled and slurred over his words, still holding Sylvia's arm in a vice-like grip.

'I know you can, just a little one. It won't hurt anyone, and something to eat, anything, anything.'

Sylvia tried to pull her arm away, but he was a strong man and he wasn't showing any signs of backing off. Her legs were shaking, she had beads of sweat on her brow and she felt so sick she thought she was going to vomit all over him, which, a tiny part of her brain thought, might be the only thing that would make him back off.

He started to ramble then, incoherent strings of words that made no sense to her, and when, out of sheer desperation she thought she just might have to scream to draw attention, she heard the lift doors open and the friendly voice of Eric, one of the porters, shout out, 'It's only me, Staff, come to collect your dirty laundry skips.'

He walked around the corner to the desk area and pulled up short when he saw what was in front of him. He reacted immediately.

'Now, now, Gordon, what you up to, then?' and to Sylvia's enormous relief, he walked up to the man and put an arm across his shoulders.

'What you doing up on these wards again, eh? You know what the police said last time, that you had to stop doing this. You can't keep wandering in here and scaring all the nice nurses now, can you?'

Sylvia felt weak with relief, and almost close to tears, as Eric, who obviously knew the man, pulled his hand off her arm and said, 'Are you OK, Staff? I guess you haven't had the pleasure of meeting Gordon?'

'No, we definitely haven't had the pleasure, Eric.'

'He's harmless enough. He's the local vagrant. Calls in here a couple of times a year, on his travels. He's usually found on the antenatal clinic, sleeping it off on one of the couches by the cleaning ladies.

'I'll see if I can find him a sandwich or two and escort him off the premises,' and shepherding the lumbering giant like a lamb, Eric restored order once more to the postnatal floor. As the lift door closed behind them, Heather came out of the bottom nursery and walked up the corridor to join Sylvia at the desk.

'You OK love? You look a bit uptight.'

Sylvia, still feeling shaky, told Heather what had just occurred.

'I've seen him before. He knows that the main entrance doors open and close automatically day and night, triggered by movement sensors, so if he's in the area, he pays us a visit. He's harmless really. If you stand up to him, he backs off immediately. It's a shame. He's spent most of his life living under hedgerows.'

Sylvia was beginning to calm down a little and, after a cup of tea, resumed her duties. She'd never thought about being vulnerable in the maternity block, but that night's experience made her more wary and careful. It triggered conversations amongst the senior staff about the vulnerability of the night shift sometimes alone on a ward when their support colleague went on a meal break. It also raised the issue of potential baby abduction from a ward, a mother's and a Midwife's worst nightmare.

Chapter Seventeen

'She's an accident waiting to happen! She can talk the talk, but not walk the walk! Last week she had the audacity to walk out of Sister Frenchit's office in the middle of another telling-off for not bothering to attend to a patient's needs. Sister Frenchit was so apoplectic; it was like seeing a verbal tsunami erupt. This student has no empathy, makes things up to suit herself, and tells lies, and I could go on.'

The Supervisor of Midwives was talking to Mrs O'Neil in her office in the Maternity Unit's training school. The student Midwife under discussion was Stella Steel and this was not the first discussion about her lack of progress and very poor people skills. Mrs O'Neil had dealt with many students over the years who had not been able to acquire the competencies required to practise Midwifery. She recognised that not all who started their training would finish it, even though extra support and teaching would be offered, so it was no surprise to hear that Miss Steel was not achieving her outcomes. What really disturbed her were the other complaints about the student's complete lack of people skills and the lying; a dangerous combination in any profession. A number of Midwives who had worked alongside Stella were all saying the same thing: this woman, even with extra training, was not fit to be entered onto the roll of practising Midwives.

Mrs O'Neil sighed, stubbed out her fourth cigarette of the day on the ashtray on her desk, and took off her gold-rimmed glasses. She placed them on the desk in front of her and wearily rubbed her eyes.

'The Central Midwives Board has very specific educational requirements that must be fulfilled if she wishes to be added to the register. If she's not achieving these competencies, then she will not be admitted to the register. She's failing on two levels as she obviously has a problem with relating to the patients' needs. From what I hear, her interpersonal skills are nil. I take it extra training and mentorship have been put in place and completed?'

The Supervisor of Midwives nodded and produced some documents showing what extra support and teaching opportunities had been provided to help her and she pushed them across the desk towards Mrs O'Neil.

'I feel we have come to the end of the line with her, and I feel really sad that we haven't been able to turn her deficits around. But the bottom line is, is she safe, would I be happy to trust her with a patient's care, and would she ask for help if she wasn't sure? And the answer to all of those questions is no. I feel there is no alternative but to terminate her training.'

Mrs O'Neil was in complete agreement, although, like the Supervisor of Midwives, she felt sad that one less Midwife would be qualifying. But protecting the lives of mothers and babies through good practice was paramount, and her job was to produce a workforce that was capable of doing that.

'Well, she's not even going to complete Part One of her training. If she had completed the first eighteen months required, then I suppose we could have awarded her a certificate to say she had completed a course of instruction, but nothing more. Without evidence showing she has completed Part One, there's no way she can move on and start Part Two.'

'I'll set up a meeting with her which I would like you to attend. I'll let you know details shortly, and let's do it sooner rather than later, shall we?'

At the same time that the meeting was taking place

in Mrs O'Neil's office, Stella Steel was on a mission. She had just entered the nurses' home block, a huge towering building that was part of the Victorian workhouse complex built over one hundred years ago. On the ground floor was an enormous sitting-room, kitchen and laundry. There was also a large wooden, wall-mounted unit placed in the main entrance. It was compartmentalised for each student's mail. There was going to be a batch of very specific mail delivered any day now and there was something she needed. She checked the cubby-holes to see if what she required had been delivered yet. It hadn't, but no worries, her need would definitely be fulfilled soon and it would pave the way for her future.

Sylvia, Rosie and Penny were across the hospital site in the queue for the staff canteen, waiting to be served a hot meal, which they would eat in record time, as usual, before dashing back to the ward areas they worked on. They were chattering excitedly, planning and organising the details of their forthcoming trip. They had all applied to attend a week-long training event, fully paid for by the hospital's training fund, which enabled Midwives to be sent on a variety of courses throughout their careers, allowing them to be kept up-to-date in the latest research and practice techniques. They had all been chosen to attend a course of instruction that would update them on the teaching of parentcraft classes; a service offered to all pregnant women from twenty-eight weeks of pregnancy until they delivered. The training would be taking place in a large hotel in Blackpool, where other Midwives from around the country would also be attending, allowing networking and the sharing of ideas.

Continuing, ongoing education was firmly embedded into Midwives' working lives, and not only was it necessary to keep up-to-date, they also had to prove it to their Supervisor. A minimum number of post-training education events was required every year by every Midwife, who would submit the information to her manager and her Supervisor. All costs would be met by the hospital..

To save on travel costs they would all travel together, using one car, and Penny, Rosie and Sylvia were feeling like they were going on holiday rather than attending a course of professional instruction. They returned to the maternity building that had become almost their second home, planning the details of their excursion.

Stella Steel was furious. That old bag, Sister Frenchit, had just given her another dressing-down, not in the privacy of her office this time but in full view of everyone on the Ward. A drip inserted into the arm of a woman she was helping to care for had been allowed to run through completely without her noticing. Another woman, with an indwelling urine catheter bag in place because her bladder had been battered by a traumatic delivery, had been asking Stella if she could please get someone to change the bag, as it was so full. She hadn't, and the bag had leaked, resulting in urine spillage all over the floor by the patient's bed. And to make matters worse, she had then proceeded to pour a woman's urine sample into the wrong twenty-four-hour collecting jar, resulting in two almost full demijohns of urine collections having to be discarded as neither were now accurate.

As she ranted and raved, Stella stood, arms crossed, the words of admonishment barely denting her armour-clad disdain of the woman in front of her. She wasn't upset about the fact that she had provided very inadequate care to her patients; in fact she couldn't have cared less. It was purely about winning or losing, regardless of what the challenge was. Her biggest kick was control, making things happen, then standing back and waiting to see the result. As Sister Frenchit's tirade continued, she thought about the time in the nursery a few months before, when she was working on one of the postnatal floors. She had been sent to the nursery to placate a crying baby who just wouldn't be settled. The baby's continuous, high-pitched crying did not create in her any maternal instinct to pick up, soothe, and murmur quiet words of comfort.

She stared at the screwed-up face, the crying reverberating inside her skull like someone hitting it with a hammer. Without conscious thought, she put her fingers over the baby's nose and compressed both nostrils shut. The crying stopped immediately. A blessed peaceful silence ensued. She watched, fascinated, as the baby's pallor changed from pink to blue and the frantically waving arms became still.

Suddenly the door to the nursery was pushed open, and a cheery voice from the nursery nurse shouted down the room to her 'Are you OK? I see you've managed to calm her.'

Stella rapidly removed her fingers and within seconds she could see the baby's colour becoming pink again.

'You've obviously got the right touch,' said the nursery nurse, 'so can I ask you to feed this other baby for me?'

When the verbal avalanche had abated, Sister

Frenchit informed Stella that Mrs O'Neil wanted to see her in her office at two o clock and under no circumstances was she to be late. With no acknowledgement, Stella stormed off the Ward, not forgetting to retrieve the watch she had found in the bathroom.

Two hours later, and deliberately fifteen minutes late, Stella knocked on Mrs O'Neil's office door, the only conformity of behaviour that she adhered to during that day. A voice called out 'Come in' and she pushed the door open and entered.

Chapter Eighteen

Sylvia, Rosie and Penny joined the huge throng of participants all arriving, it seemed, at the sea-front hotel at the same time. They met up at the foyer's desk to book into their rooms and register for their training week. They would all be sharing one huge room and, as Penny commented, 'It's like being back on the district, doing our community placement.' It would be the first of many opportunities to access good quality training throughout their careers and they all looked forward to a week of learning, which would become a regular and necessary part of their working lives.

They signed the register, pinned on their badges and prepared to enjoy the company and friendship of those colleagues who had accompanied them, and also to appreciate the feeling of solidarity that bound them together as they mingled with Midwives who came from the four corners of the British Isles and from other countries too. Later that night, in the hotel bar, they sat discussing the day's events, fascinated by the conversations they had had with other Midwives who practised their skills in foreign parts. There was no period of introduction required or needed as they enthusiastically exchanged stories and experiences. The rapport with each other was instantaneous. The three Midwives topped up their glasses and proposed a toast. They raised their glasses in unison.

'Here's to the 72–74 set. May they never lose touch.' And they never did.

At the same time, a young student Midwife was in the sitting-room of the nurses' home, crying, and being comforted by her colleagues.

'Look, Stephanie, it's probably just late. Post gets delayed all the time. You know what it's like.'

'I know that, but how come I'm the only one who hasn't received theirs? All of you lot have got yours. I must have failed,' and she burst into a fresh bout of crying.

Three hundred and fifty miles away, in another Midwifery training school, a meeting was taking place. Part Two, the last six months of Midwifery training, was being planned for by the tutors. In front of them they had a list of the successful Part One candidates who would be completing their training in six months' time. All of the names were known to them, except one. A query from one of the tutors elicited a response from the other.

'Oh, yes, she's recently moved house. She's just completed her Part One. I have her certificate here. She will be joining the group – a Miss Stephanie Carter. Her references look quite excellent.'

Epilogue

Light as a feather, the razor-sharp scalpel gently touched the anaesthetised woman's skin. A tiny pinprick of blood appeared and blossomed as the scalpel was drawn skilfully in a straight line across the woman's abdomen, just above the Symphysis Pubis joint. The surgeon repeated the manoeuvre, using just a little more pressure, so that the sharp blade could separate the layers of creamy, white fat that lay just beneath the skin, and there was plenty of that.

The Midwife assisting him used the suction apparatus to clear away the blood as it seeped out of severed vessels. The diathermy rod that used heat to seal off small bleeding blood vessels gave off its distinctive smell of burning flesh as he worked his way through the layers of skin, fat and fascia. Abdominal muscle was exposed beneath sheets of connective tissue. He marvelled at the ingenuity of the interlocking layers that created a strong, muscular girdle, allowing complex movement of the torso. The Rectus

Abdominis muscle that ran from its attachment on the sternum and ribs, straight down in a flat sheath to be attached to the hip bones at the front, had already started to separate midline, longitudinally, as the ever-enlarging uterus and its contents had put extra pressure on its attachments as pregnancy had advanced.

He used the fingers of both hands to separate further and enlarge the opening of Rectus Abdominis, exposing the peritoneum, or thin skin, covering the outside of the uterus and all other internal organs inside a human body. Thick swabs, with tapes attached that could ensure where they were at all times when inside the body cavity, were used to mop up blood as it pooled beneath his fingers, allowing a clearer view of the organ he was about to cut into.

An opaque, white, glistening layer of peritoneum covering the outside of the uterus, ensuring there was no friction between it and other organs or body parts nearby, came into view. He gently pushed loops of intestine to one side, out of the way of his scalpel. Even a small cut into the intestines would create huge problems of infection and immobility of the gut, lethal in some cases he had seen. He never tired of seeing the organ that was, in his mind, its own complete universe. A universe inside another anatomical universe, he contemplated. How many other humans had the privilege of seeing that every day?

He incised quickly through the thin, tissue-like peritoneum, and reached the body of the uterus. He made his incision. Liquor gushed out with a spurt and the Midwife sucked it out of the way as he quickly inserted his hand into the cavity and found a plump leg. He grabbed hold of it and pulled it free through the gap in the uterus he had just cut open. He found the other leg easily and, grasping the baby by both its ankles, started to ease the body out of the uterus, legs, bottom, body, chest, emerging into the outside world.

It was a good-sized baby and he had to perform some more manoeuvring to deliver the head, the Midwife inserting a suction tube into the baby's mouth before he had freed it completely. At last the baby was free and out. He quickly clamped and cut the cord and the assisting Midwife wrapped the baby in a towel and handed him over to the waiting Paediatrician. Drugs were given to help the patient's uterus contract and shear off its wall the placenta, a huge dinner-plate size mass, aesthetically ugly but beautiful in its complexity. He grasped the cord end and removed the organ whose function was responsible for every life on the planet he inhabited.

The Midwife had already laid out a collection of

suturing materials and had threaded up a variety of needles. He spent the next twenty-five minutes or so suturing back the layers of the uterus he had just cut open, ensuring that any leaking blood vessels were securely closed off.

Before he started to suture the abdominal corset, he located the thin, white hair-like structures attached each side at the top of the uterus, running horizontally out towards the ovaries – the fallopian tubes. They provided a highway on each side for the fertilised egg to travel on its five-day journey back to the uterus, searching for the life-giving blood supply. It would snuggle down into the vascular layers of the uterus, much like newly hatched chicks that burrowed under the feathers of a mother hen. The highway of life, he mused, a highway of fertility leading to the most sophisticated and complex nest of all.

He was handed on request two sets of forceps that he attached to one of the fallopian tubes, repeating the process each side. He cut in between each set of forceps, ensuring that no more sperm or ova could pass from any direction along the tube. Secure suturing of the cut ends effectively ended the woman's reproductive life. The tubal ligation complete, he put sutures into the abdominal muscle layers, and finally closed with sutures to fat and skin.

The woman's abdomen was swabbed again and he stepped back from the theatre bed, allowing his support staff to take over as he de-scrubbed in the sink area, taking off his gown, mask and gloves.

Before leaving the theatre, he picked up the woman's notes, and then settled down in the relative peace and quiet of the doctors' sitting-room, where he grabbed a drink and prepared to complete his record keeping.

He scanned the woman's history again. A drug addict, an alcoholic, seven previous pregnancies with six children under the care of Social Services, the seventh under the care of a grandmother.

He meticulously documented the procedure he had just carried out, omitting completely the fact that he had also performed a tubal ligation without the woman's request or knowledge. He had not the slightest qualm about carrying out a procedure that would ensure no further suffering of unwanted pregnancies, and no more maltreated babies on the at-risk register. He closed the notes, put on his white coat and walked around to the antenatal clinic where he had a long list of patients waiting to see him. Mr Baxter was a Consultant with an impeccable reputation and was, as always, in demand.

About The Author

Sylvia Baddeley is a retired Midwife with forty-plus years of clinical practice. The death of her sister-in-law from a ruptured aortic aneurysm the day after her daughter was born was the catalyst that had driven her to enter the world of Midwifery.

Her career spans a journey that includes pioneering Aquanatal classes in the UK and lecturing locally, nationally and internationally at a number of Midwifery conferences as well as teaching exercise to music classes as part of her Midwifery role. She acted as advisor to London Central YMCA's video on exercise during pregnancy and published a book called *Health Related Fitness During Pregnancy*. She was also Midwife advisor on Desmond Morris's video called Baby Watching.

Throughout her career she published many articles in Midwifery journals. She also qualified as an aromatherapist, reflexologist, and body masseuse, as well as becoming a baby massage instructor. She integrated all of these skills into her Midwifery practice. Her work in a local Sure Start programme offered opportunities for multi-agency working and for the development of her role as a Bonding and Attachment Specialist. In this capacity she was invited to afternoon tea in the gardens of Number Ten Downing Street.

Sylvia is also a familiar voice on local radio and her first book in this series called *Push! Close Encounters Of The Midwife Kind* was long-listed for the annual Arnold Bennett Award in 2021.

Made in the USA
Middletown, DE
11 August 2023